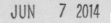

Tuesday, August 13, 9:47 p.m

I'd call 911

If they could help

They can't

Today was an unfortunate mix of surprisingly good and the kind of bad you never quite get over. I'd start with the good, but I'm so traumatized by tonight's horrible ending that it's all I can think about. It was the most embarrassing moment to date of my thirteen-year-almost-four-month existence, which is saying lot, because I've suffered a lot of embarrassing moments. But they all pale in comparison to what happened tonight. I'll get to the beginning of the story in a minute, but the main point is that my best friend heard, smelled, and practically saw my dad take a dump.

It was even more horrible than it sounds.

The whole thing started this afternoon when my mom called Bryan's mom to see if the Stephensons wanted to go with us to try the Crawfish Cafe. It's not that often that anything opens in Faraway, Alabama, especially a new restaurant, so everyone was excited to try it. Particularly Dad. Actually, he was more than excited. In the car on the way to the restaurant, he was literally blabbering the whole way about the restaurant business and how hard it is to get it right, and how the Crawfish Cafe originated in New Orleans and is a big hit there. "I'm anxious to

THE MOSTLY MISERABLE LIFE
OF APRIL SINCLAIR

Too Good to Be True

LAURIE FRIEDMAN

MINNEAPOLIS

Darby Creek
A division of Lerner Publishing Group, Inc.
241 First Avenue North
Minneapolis, MN 55401 USA

For reading levels and more information, look up this title
at www.lernerbooks.com.

Main body text set in Janson Text LT Std 12/17.
Typeface provided by Linotype AG.

Library of Congress Cataloging-in-Publication Data

Friedman, Laurie B., 1964–
        Too good to be true / by Laurie Friedman.
            pages   cm. — (The mostly miserable life of April Sinclair ; #2)
        Summary: Diaries entries record eighth-grader April's attempts to fix
    her friendships new and old.
        ISBN 978–1–4677–0926–2 (trade hard cover : alk. paper)
        ISBN 978–1–4677–2422–7 (eBook)
        [1. Friendship—Fiction. 2. Dating (Social customs)—Fiction.
    3. Interpersonal relations—Fiction. 4. Diaries—Fiction.] I. Title.
    PZ7.F89773To 2014
    [Fic]—dc23   2013026434

Manufactured in the United States of America
1 – BP – 7/15/14

For Becca and Adam.
Truly the best kids ever.

This is a new year. A new beginning. And things will change.

—*Taylor Swift*

Tuesday, August 13, 9:47 P.M.
I'd call 911
If they could help
They can't

Today was an unfortunate mix of surprisingly good and the kind of bad you never quite get over. I'd start with the good, but I'm so traumatized by tonight's horrible ending that it's all I can think about. It was the most embarrassing moment to date of my thirteen-year-almost-four-month existence, which is saying a lot, because I've suffered a lot of embarrassing moments. But they all pale in comparison to what happened tonight. I'll get to the beginning of the story in a minute, but the main point is that my best friend heard, smelled, and practically saw my dad take a dump.

It was even more horrible than it sounds.

The whole thing started this afternoon when my mom called Brynn's mom to see if the Stephenses wanted to go with us to try the Crawfish Cafe. It's not that often that anything opens in Faraway, Alabama, especially a new restaurant, so everyone was excited to try it. Particularly Dad. Actually, he was more than excited. In the car on the way to the restaurant, he was literally blabbering the whole way about the restaurant business and how hard it is to get it right, and how the Crawfish Cafe originated in New Orleans and is a big hit there. "I'm anxious to see what they did with the place," he told Mom.

May and June and I were in the backseat. May leaned forward. "Dad, why do you care what they did with the place?"

"Yeah, Dad, why do you care what they did with the place?" repeated June.

Dad smiled into the rearview mirror and shrugged like he suddenly didn't want to seem so anxious. "They're our competition now," he explained. "There are a limited number of dining-out dollars in Faraway, and I want to make sure I know what the Love Doctor Diner is up against."

Now that Dad owns a restaurant, I get why he thought it was important to check out the competition. What I didn't get was how weird he acted once we got to the Crawfish Cafe.

The minute we sat down, Dad started ordering food like he had a serious case of the munchies. "We'll have the crawfish," Dad said with a smile. He ordered it every way they offered it. Boiled. Sautéed. Étouffée. Gumbo. Beignets.

Mom gave Dad her I-don't-think-that's-such-a-good-idea look, but Dad kept going.

"We'd also like the fried shrimp, the crab bisque, and the lobster pie," he told the waitress.

She raised an eyebrow. Brynn's parents looked at each other. "We can come back, Rex," Mom said gently.

But Dad was a train that couldn't be stopped. He ordered sides and salads like the end of the world was near.

When the food came, Dad was even more jacked than when he ordered. He was eating everything, and he wasn't even talking to anyone at the table. Food was going in. Crumbs were flying out. People at the next table were staring at him.

I could tell Mom thought he should slow down. "Owning and managing the diner can be stressful," she said to the Stephenses like that justified his behavior. But I knew what she was really trying to do was send Dad a message to STOP EATING LIKE A PIG! Even my little sisters thought he was over the top.

"Dad, you better slow down or you're going to get a tummy ache," said May.

"Yeah, Dad, you're going to get a tummy ache," repeated June. I don't like how, at age seven, June continues to repeat everything she hears, but she was justified in saying what she did.

I decided to ignore the human shovel at our table and started talking to Brynn about eighth grade, which starts next Monday. At some point while Brynn and I were discussing what shoes we wanted to get, Dad left the table. I didn't know where he was going. I was just relieved he was taking his hyper energy with him. I think everyone else was too.

"April, how do you feel about starting eighth grade?" Brynn's dad asked me. Brynn and I have been best friends since kindergarten, and Mr. Stephens always calls me his other daughter.

"It has to be better than being in sixth or seventh grade," I told him. He laughed like he understood where I was coming from.

Then Brynn said she's excited for this year because she's the editor of the school paper and can't wait to "speak the journalistic truth," and then our moms jumped in, saying that they can't believe we're in our last year of middle school. Brynn's mom actually got teary-eyed as they were talking. That's when Brynn pinched my leg, which I knew was my cue for us to get up and go to the bathroom.

It's also when my nightmare began.

Brynn and I left the table and went down the hall to the door that had a big sign that said Crawladies. Right when we walked in, there was a terrible smell. I actually thought I might pass out. I pointed to the stall where it was coming from, and Brynn waved her hand in front of her nose, trying to clear her airspace.

Then we heard a sound—more like a string of sounds. A grunt, a few groans, and then . . . I don't even want to write this. The person in the stall had terrible diarrhea, and Brynn and I heard the whole thing. I looked at Brynn. Even though the bathroom smelled disgusting, it was pretty funny listening to what was coming out of the stall. Brynn put her hand over her mouth to keep from laughing. I tried to cover my mouth too, but I started laughing. I couldn't stop myself. "We should go," I tried to say quietly to Brynn, but I guess it wasn't quiet enough because the other person in the bathroom heard me.

"April?" said a voice from inside the stall. I froze. It was bad enough that the voice coming from inside the stall said my name. But it was even worse that the voice seemed to be coming from a man. A man I know!

Brynn's jaw dropped. "April, is that your dad?" she said.

And the next thing I knew, he walked out of the stall and there we all were. Me, my best friend, and my dad who'd just had a serious case of the runs. He seemed confused. "What are you girls doing in the men's room?" he asked.

Brynn was speechless. I wasn't! "Dad, this is the ladies room! The sign on the door said Crawladies."

My dad actually nodded and sort of half-smiled like that explanation made sense. "I guess I was in too big of a hurry. I thought the sign said Crawdaddies. I'm sorry, girls," he said. Then he turned on the faucet to wash his hands, like that apology could make up for what just happened.

But here's a fact: there's nothing he could have done (or can ever do) that could make up for what happened in the ladies room tonight!

I mean, in what world (except for mine) does your dad eat too much, crap his brains out in front of your best friend, and then act like it was no big deal? Shouldn't a responsible father of three know NOT to do that sort of thing? And who eats so much so fast that they don't even take the time to read a simple sign? I was mortified and horribly grossed out and still am. Brynn was too. She's my best friend, but even a friend who has been around as long as she has shouldn't have to experience what she did. I just have two words to describe tonight: IT STUNK!

I was so upset that I forgot to write about the surprisingly good thing that happened today: Billy and I had our one-month anniversary! Billy texted me early this morning (at 6:04 A.M. to be exact) to say happy anniversary. What he actually texted was "Hey BFGF, guess who I thought of as soon as I woke up? Can't believe it has been a month."

If most boys texted something like that, especially at 6:04 in the morning, it would seem kind of stalkerish. But it didn't seem creepy at all when it came from Billy. It seemed like he meant it, and that's what's so cool about Billy. He's fine saying exactly what he feels. Like calling me his Best Friend Girl Friend and saying, "Who wouldn't want both rolled into one?" I love that he thinks about me that way. I also love how we celebrated our anniversary.

We went on a bike ride and then for ice cream, and when we got back to Billy's house, he gave me the giant-sized Hershey's kiss his parents brought him back from their trip to New York this summer. "All my kisses are for you, April Sinclair," he said. Then he kissed me and laughed.

It made me laugh too. I knew he was just joking around, but it was sweet. "You're so weird," I said.

Billy poked me in the ribs, which tickled. "Weird in a good way, I hope."

I nodded, smiling. Then Billy said he had another present for me. He gave me a stuffed bear with a big yellow bow around its neck. "We're going to call him Rat," Billy said.

"What kind of name is that for a bear?" I asked.

"It's a perfect name for this bear because it looks more like a rat than a bear. And the other name I thought of, Mr. Snuggles, didn't suit him at all."

I looked at the bear and saw exactly what he meant. "Why would you give me a bear that looks like a rat?" I asked Billy.

"Any guy could give you a bear that looks like

a bear, but where would you ever find another boyfriend that would give you a bear that looks like a rat?"

It made perfect sense, and at that moment, sitting on Billy's bed, I knew I loved Rat and I knew I loved having a boyfriend who doesn't do what most people do.

Friday, August 16, 6:45 P.M.
Just home from Gaga's

My grandmother called an emergency family meeting this afternoon. Everyone in my family dropped whatever it was they were doing and rushed to her house, where she announced that her bridge group had decided it was time to do something different, so they started the Happiness Movement. "We're on a crusade to help people find their inner peace," Gaga said.

I didn't see how Gaga and her lady friends could suddenly become poster children for happiness, and I don't think anyone else did either. "It sounds like a weird cult," said my cousin Harry, who's in tenth grade and is probably a two out of ten on the happiness scale.

"I think she's starting to lose it," mumbled my Uncle Dusty.

"Mom, do you need to go to a hospital?" asked my Aunt Lila, getting up to take a closer look at Gaga.

"Why do we all need to be here?" my Uncle Drew wanted to know. He stood up, ready to leave.

Gaga asked us all to sit and then started answering our questions. "I've never felt better," she said. "And the last thing I need is a hospital. The reason I wanted all of my children and grandchildren here for this announcement is because what I'm about to say affects each one of you personally."

I have two aunts, two uncles, four first cousins, and two sisters plus my own parents, and I could tell that not one of these people had any clue how Gaga's announcement affected them personally. But we didn't have to wait long to find out.

"My dear family, I've been playing the same card game with the same ladies for the last twenty-three years, and it took us all this time to discover the meaning of life, which is that everyone should be happy."

My Uncle Dusty looked at my Uncle Drew and rolled his eyes. I think they both feel like they took on a crazy lady in Gaga when they married my aunts, and to be fair, their views are somewhat warranted.

My cousin Harry raised his hand. "How can you just be happy?" he asked.

But Gaga had an explanation for that too. "Choose to be positive," said Gaga. "Positive attitude plus positive action makes you part of the Happiness Movement." Then she told us that out of the goodness of her heart and her inherent faith in each of us to lead our lives in a positive manner, she was going to go ahead and make everyone in our family members of the Happiness Movement.

Harry told Gaga he didn't want to be a member especially if there were any hidden membership fees or weird initiation rituals, but Gaga assured him there were no fees, only free T-shirts. With that, Gaga opened up a big box that was sitting on her dining room table and started taking out bright yellow T-shirts with a big happy face on the front and lettering on the back that said, "Proud member of the Happiness Movement."

She made us all put them on before we left, but no one was happy about it.

"I hate bright yellow," said my cousin Amanda.

Uncle Drew shook his head like there was no way he was wearing that T-shirt.

Even my aunts and my mom, who always try to be patient with Gaga, weren't too happy about it. "Mom, don't you think this is a bit much?" Aunt Lilly asked.

But Gaga just said, "Part of being positive is ignoring the naysayers." Then she announced that my cousins Charlotte and Izzy were to accompany her on Saturday to Winn-Dixie, where she and the other members of the Happiness Movement will be spreading their message of positivity.

As we left, Gaga asked each one of us to please say what we were happy about. I told her I'd have to get back to her on that one. I didn't think she'd like hearing that what I was happy about was that I didn't have to go to Winn-Dixie with Charlotte and Izzy on Saturday.

Sunday, August 18, 10:45 P.M.
Where I am: at my desk
Where I should be: in my bed

I can't sleep. School starts in the morning, and even though my brain doesn't have to officially start thinking until 8:30 A.M. tomorrow, it's working overtime right now. So many thoughts are flying through my head. Mostly, what this year will be like. I really want it to be good, but it's hard to imagine it will be when I think about how badly seventh grade ended.

It's like a loop that keeps playing in my head.

Billy kissed me. I told Brynn. She got mad, but she got over it. Billy found out I told Brynn, and *he* got mad. Then Matt Parker (who had just moved in next door) kissed me. To top things off, my parents made me stay home from camp and go on a family vacation, because they didn't like the way I was acting. Billy and Brynn went to camp without me, and I had no clue what they were doing or saying or what things would be like when they got back. But then they came home, and everything with Brynn was cool, and Billy asked me to be his girlfriend. It was like I snapped my fingers and everything instantly changed from bad to good and it's been mostly that way ever since.

I think about what Gaga said about being part of the Happiness Movement. It sounds kind of stupid, but I've actually been happy for the past month, and it would be nice to stay that way. But how do you do that? Is there a way to make this a good year? If I have a positive attitude and act positively, will I just stay happy?

The good news is that I have things to be happy about, like a great boyfriend, a great best friend, and two boobs that are the same size. This wasn't always the case. About two weeks ago, I went to bed one night and it's like my left boob decided to catch up with my right one while I was sleeping.

I credit my sister June and Greek yogurt for this awesome change. June told me she read that Kim Kardashian eats Greek yogurt. Why my seven-year-old sister was reading anything about Kim Kardashian, I don't know. But when June told me Kim eats yogurt, I did a very simple analysis.

Kim has a big butt (in a good way).

Kim eats yogurt.

I have no butt.

I eat no yogurt.

I want a butt like Kim's.

I need to eat yogurt.

It made perfect sense. So I started eating Greek yogurt every morning for breakfast. It didn't give me the butt I was hoping for, but my left boob caught up with my right one and the only thing that changed was what I was eating.

I should take this as a sign that my life has turned a corner and I'm entering the happy phase. Maybe there's an old me and a new me. The old me would have worried that writing that sort of thing would bring me bad luck. But the new me just needs to stay positive and believe that if I do, good things will happen. Why not? My boob grew! What are the odds of that? Maybe when someone goes through a phase like I did this summer where everything went wrong, whoever it is that's dishing out the things-going-wrong stuff realizes you've had your share and it's time to move on to someone else.

Who knows? But that's my theory and I, April Elizabeth Sinclair, am sticking with it.

Up, Up, Up!
It's going to be a big, big, big day!

—Effie Trinket

Monday, August 19, 7:23 A.M.
At my ~~desk~~ neat and tidy desk

Day one. Grade eight. I'm starting the year with a positive attitude and positive action. Last night, I cleaned off my desk, organized my backpack, laid out my clothes, and made plans for where to meet Billy and Brynn before school. I slept with my straightening iron in my bed so May couldn't find it, hide it, and get me in trouble for yelling at her for hiding my things. This morning, I woke up early; straightened my hair; ate oatmeal for breakfast; and after I had brushed my teeth, I looked in the mirror and said, "It's going to be a great day!" I probably sounded like an ad for Folgers coffee. But I don't care.

As long as it works.

4:47 P.M.
Back at my desk

Maybe there's something to be said for positivity. I tried being positive all day, and to be honest, I've had worse first days back to school. I'm sure I could find things to complain about, like having first-period PE, which meant that by the time I'd finished playing forty minutes of field hockey, there was absolutely no point in straightening my hair this morning.

Or having second-period science with Mrs. Thompson, whose classroom is an unair-conditioned trailer at the back of the campus. By the time I walked there and sat through another forty minutes, I not only had frizzy hair, but I also didn't smell my freshest.

I could complain about having to walk (0.3 miles according to my Trail Tracker app) from Mrs. Thompson's class to third-period assembly and getting even hotter than I already was, or about having fourth-period lunch, which started at 10:47 and which meant I was expected to eat meatloaf or chicken patties before I'd even finished digesting my oatmeal.

I could also complain that even though I had fourth-period lunch with Billy and Brynn, I had no classes with Billy and only study hall and fifth-period math with Brynn, which really didn't seem fair especially since Billy and Brynn had second, seventh, and eighth periods together, which means I could definitely complain about the fact that Faraway Middle School doesn't let students request who they want to be in class with.

But I'm going to resist the temptation to complain about any of those things (and some other things) since I'm the new, positive me. And in my positive view, today was pretty good. It wasn't like there was a whole string of good things that happened, but there was one thing that happened and if it works out the way I want it to, it would be great.

During assembly, a bunch of teachers were making announcements about clubs and activities. Ms. Baumann was there—the dance team coach from the high school—and she announced that she's opening up four spots for eighth-grade girls on the dance team. She said there are a lot of juniors and seniors on the team, and she wants to "nurture young talent." Tryouts are going to be next Thursday, and the girls who make it will go to the high school every day after school to practice with the team, and they'll perform with the team in competitions and in the fall dance show just before Thanksgiving. They'll even get to perform at homecoming!

When she finished talking, the gym got really noisy. It seemed like every single girl got excited about it. The Faraway High School dance team is amazing, and being part of homecoming and the fall dance show (which is a huge deal in town) would be so cool. Emily Pope, who has taken dance for years and was sitting two rows in front of me, started clapping and cheering like crazy. She'll definitely make the team.

Brynn, who was sitting next to me, reached over and squeezed my hand hard like she had breaking news. "We have to make it!" she whispered.

I squeezed back. We've always talked about how cool it would be to be on the dance team together. "We need to start practicing," I said to Brynn as we were leaving the assembly. She nodded like she agreed completely.

After the assembly, a bunch of girls were talking about trying out, and Brynn was quiet. I know Brynn better than anyone, and the only time she's quiet is when she's mad or scared. Today she didn't have anything to be mad about, which means she got scared about tryouts and making the team. She must really want it. I do too.

I know I'm supposed to be embracing the new me and staying positive, so I'll just say this: I'm excited about trying out for the dance team, but I'll be a lot more excited if I make it.

5:42 P.M.

Mom just asked me if I'd walk Gilligan before dinner. The old me would have done it, but I would have groaned and rolled my eyes when Mom asked me to do it. The new me took the leash without complaint.

5:57 P.M.

I'm back from my walk, and I have a

question: how am I supposed to stay positive when I'm doing something as uncomplicated as walking my dog and something happens that complicates it?

While I was walking Gilligan, I ran into Matt Parker, who was also walking his dog. This isn't the first time this has happened. It happens a lot and it's weird! I know if I talked to Brynn about it, she'd say, "It's not so weird. Matt's got a dog and a mom who probably makes him walk his dog before dinner just like your mom makes you walk your dog, and he lives next door to you." But a) it feels weird to me, like Matt's watching out his window and when he sees me walking my dog, he walks his too, and b) I couldn't talk to Brynn about it anyway. Not after what happened this summer. Matt Parker is one topic that's off-limits with Brynn. Whatever. The problem is that I'm always a mental case around Matt. Like just now. He started walking beside me and telling me all this stuff about high school and how it's so much cooler than middle school.

I could have said a bunch of normal things back, like, *"Cool,"* or *"Awesome."* But what I said was "My mom is waiting for me to serve dinner and I have to go."

When I said that, Matt did this head bob thing he always does when he's done with a conversation. Then he turned around and walked back to his house.

Why would I say I had to go? I meant that I had to go eat dinner, but Matt could have taken it to mean I had to go to the bathroom. I sincerely hope he didn't take it that way, but why wouldn't he? I mean, at least half the time when people say they have to go, they mean they have to pee.

I can't think of one good reason why I would say anything to Matt that makes him think I have to pee. Seriously, there has to be something wrong with me. Why can't I just talk to Matt like I talk to every other human on the planet? Part of me doesn't even like talking to him, but another part does and it doesn't want to say the wrong thing. It's confusing, like feeling hot and cold or right and wrong at the same time. That sounds so stupid. I don't know why I'm so weird about Matt.

Anyway, the whole conversation took maybe a minute, but it was an uncomfortable minute. My legs actually got shaky walking next to him. Next time Mom asks me to walk Gilligan, I'm going to tell her to ask May to do it. Or maybe I won't. I don't know. Trying to decide makes me feel much more like the old April than the new, positive one.

10:02 P.M.
In bed

I was just on the phone with Billy and Dad came into my room and we had the most annoying conversation.

Dad: April, you look tired.

Me (to Billy): Hold on.

Me (to Dad): How would you know? You don't have your glasses on.

Dad: Lights out.

Me: Dad!

Dad: April!

But the fact that dad is overbearing and half-blind is not the point. The point is that I love talking to Billy. He's the only person I never get sick of talking to. Whenever I hang up after talking to him, I look at my phone to see how long we talked. Tonight was fifty-three minutes. Our record is ninety-four minutes.

Thinking about talking to Billy makes me think about talking to Matt today. I really don't know why I'm thinking about talking to Matt. I talked to Matt for one bad minute and Billy for fifty-three good ones.

The worst part of success is trying to find someone who is happy for you.

—*Bette Midler*

Thursday, August 22, 5:35 P.M.

In my garage

Brynn just left. Practice for dance team tryouts officially started this afternoon in my garage. Brynn and I tried practicing yesterday and the day before, but somehow on both days May and June ended up in the garage with us and they did most of the dancing. Yesterday, May said I looked like a duck when I danced and June repeated it and then they both started waddling around like ducks. So today I asked Mom if she would take them with her when she went to do her errands, and it was just Brynn and me.

Even though we really needed to practice, it was almost better when May and June were around.

This isn't going to sound like the "new" me, but I didn't enjoy practicing with Brynn. She was so annoying. She kept saying that I should straighten my arms and point my toes and keep my head up. So I said, "Brynn, you should be doing those things too."

She laughed like it was ridiculous I would say that. Then she said, "You know, I don't mean this in a mean way, but you do kind of look like a duck when you dance."

When I told her I didn't see how she could say that, she said, "I'm just reporting what I see. Besides, May and June already said it."

Whatever. I didn't like hearing it.

Friday, August 23, 5:42
In my garage, again

More dance practice in my garage.

The whole staying-positive thing is getting old fast. Brynn and I both danced to the song we're supposed to try out to. "How do I look?" Brynn asked when we finished.

I said she looked good. Then, instead of telling me I looked good back, she said, "Making the high school dance team as an eighth grader is a HUGE deal! I'm going to put an article about it

on the FRONT PAGE of the school newspaper."
She looked at me like she was waiting for the
full effect of her words to sink in. Then she said,
"April, I hope this doesn't hurt your feelings, but
it doesn't look like you're trying your hardest."
She made this long speech about the importance
of honesty and about how as my best friend, she
thought she should be brutally honest with me.
"That's just what you do with people you love,"
she said.

But she didn't have to be that honest. And if
I'm being honest, I thought I looked better than
Brynn. After she left, I called Billy. I was going
to ask him if Brynn's brutal honesty ever bothers
him, but he didn't pick up.

7:48 P.M.

We just got home from dinner at the Love
Doctor Diner. Dad wanted us all to see his new
and what he calls "improved" Love Doctor
Diner sign. It not only lights up but also changes
colors from hot pink to bright purple to fire-
engine red. It's the kind of sign you can see from
anywhere in town or, for that matter, from the

next two towns over. I almost had to shield my eyes when I looked at it.

"What do you girls think?" Dad asked as we all watched the sign flash through its color palette.

"I think it's beautiful," said May.

"I think it's beautiful," repeated June.

"April, what do you think?" Dad asked.

I thought about what Brynn said this afternoon about my dancing and how it's important to be brutally honest with people you love. Personally, I think brutal honesty is overrated.

I told Dad I thought his sign was beautiful.

Saturday, August 24, 4:45 P.M.
Just home from Brynn's
Can't believe what happened

Brynn and I spent all afternoon at her house practicing for the dance team tryouts. It was going pretty well until Billy came over. It wasn't that I didn't want to see him. I was just surprised he was there. He kind of seemed surprised he was there too. "So why did you text me to come over?" he asked Brynn.

"April and I are getting ready for the dance team tryouts. We're both going to dance to the song we're trying out to, and we want you to judge us and tell us who's the best."

I thought I was hearing things. First of all, that wasn't something "we" wanted. "We" never discussed it. I didn't even know she had texted Billy to come over. And I could tell that Billy was uncomfortable with the idea.

But before Billy or I could say anything, Brynn turned on the music and said she was going first. Her hips were moving and her arms were flying right in front of Billy and I could tell she was trying her hardest. When she finished, she looked at Billy and smiled, and then she looked at me. "April, it's your turn."

I couldn't just sit there, so I got up, started the music again, and danced. But it was uncomfortable. Even though Billy is my boyfriend, it was awkward dancing right in front of him.

When I finished, Brynn looked at Billy. "Who did you think was better?" she asked.

It was so crazy. I couldn't believe she was asking Billy to choose. I don't know if it's because she thinks she's better and she wanted him to think that too or if she's scared we won't both make the team and on some level (hopefully a subconscious one), she's trying to psyche me out. Whatever. It doesn't matter. Billy said it was an absolute tie. When Brynn insisted he had to choose, he wouldn't. All he said was "You dance differently, but you both looked good."

It made me love Billy. Not in an I'm-in-love-with-him way but just an I-love-how-he-handles-things kind of way.

9:35 P.M.

The more I think about what happened at Brynn's today, the more it bothers me. I keep thinking the reason Brynn danced in front of Billy and wanted him to choose who dances better is because she likes him. I mean, we've all been friends for a long time, so of course she likes him. But before they left for camp this summer, I thought she might have liked him as more than a friend.

She didn't, but I'm wondering: does she now?

I guess the question that matters is: does Billy like Brynn in a more-than-a-friend way? And the answer to that is no. He likes me. He's my boyfriend.

But Brynn does have shinier hair, a cuter nose, and better clothes. Does that matter? I don't think so. I don't care. Well . . . OK, I care.

Just a little.

Sunday, August 25, 3:37 P.M.
OMG!

I can NOT believe what happened this afternoon!

I was lying out in the backyard in my bikini, trying to get tan before dance tryouts, and squeezing lemons on my hair, which is supposed to give you blond highlights. Then suddenly Matt Parker walked out into his backyard, looked over the fence, saw me and walked over, and sat down on my towel next to me! He didn't even ask me if he could sit down. He just did.

I was shocked he was sitting there, and I guess I gave him a what-are-you-doing-here look, because he started explaining. "I could smell the lemons from next door. We had a lemon tree in our backyard in California. I love the smell of lemons. It reminds me of home," he said. Then, before I could do anything, he leaned over toward me. For a few seconds, I thought he was going to kiss the top of my head, but he smelled it!

"My new name for you is California," he said. He smiled the cutest smile ever, and then he got up and left.

I probably shouldn't admit this, but I laid there for a long time hoping he'd come back. I can never think of anything to say to Matt, and suddenly there were so many things I wanted to ask him, like why he moved to Faraway and if he misses California and what his family is like. But Matt didn't come back, so I'm saving my questions.

I probably shouldn't admit this either, but I like my new nickname.

It's not easy writing in a journal while you're taking a bath. It's also not easy trying to relax (which is what I'm trying to do) when dance team tryouts are tomorrow.

Brynn and I have been practicing all week. Today when we finished, Brynn was like, "Are you nervous?"

"I'm pretty nervous," I admitted. Then I asked her if she was, and she said the only thing she's nervous about is that we won't both make it. She said it like it would be a shame for me if she made it and I didn't, but I know she's just as worried that she won't make the team either.

We both really want this. I try to take a deep breath and push all negative thoughts out of my head. I think about the old me and the new me. The old me would believe I won't make it. The new me needs to think that I can.

Eenie, meenie, miney, mo.

Old me feels like the way to go.

Thursday, August 29, 1:52 P.M.
Study hall

I'm so nervous, I can't study. I don't usually study in study hall, but there's no chance I'm going to today. I just looked across the row of desks separating Brynn from me. She looked like she's pretending to study, but I know she's thinking about dance tryouts after school.

Dear God, please let me make it.

7:54 P.M.
In my room
Standing up
Too excited to sit!

I MADE IT!!! I'm going to write that again because I can. I MADE IT!!!

I can't believe I did. Tryouts were so stressful. Twenty-eight girls, four spots. Ms. Baumann broke us up into groups of four, and my group, which was Brynn, me, Emily, and this girl Heather, was last. It was torture waiting and watching all the other groups. Brynn kept telling me to try and relax even though I could tell she wasn't relaxed at all.

Heather kept saying she'd forgotten to shave her legs and asking if we thought Ms. Baumann would notice. I actually thought Brynn was going to be her truthful self and tell Heather that her black, hairy leg stubble was noticeable, but she didn't. We had to wait for over an hour for our turn, and then I was focusing so hard on the moves and pointing my toes and keeping my head up that it felt like the dance only took a few seconds, and after we danced, we had to sit around and wait another half hour while Ms. Baumann made her decisions.

I didn't think I was going to make it. I really didn't. When Ms. Baumann stood up to announce who made the team, Brynn squeezed my hand.

"There were so many good dancers, and I hope those of you who didn't make it will try out again next year," said Ms. Baumann. She looked around at all of us and then down at her list.

"Emily Pope, Kate Walls, Vanessa Mendez, and April Sinclair. Congratulations, girls, and welcome to the Faraway High School dance team."

When she finished announcing who'd made it, all the older girls started cheering. I felt Brynn let go of my hand. The next thing I knew, Emily was grabbing and hugging Kate and Vanessa and me and saying how much fun we were going to have. All the older girls were hugging us too, like we were part of their club now. As happy as I was, I wanted to find Brynn. I knew she'd be upset. I tried to wriggle out of the hugging, but it took a while, and when I finally broke free, Brynn was gone.

When I came home, I shouted the news so everyone would hear it. "I made it!" I screamed.

"You made it?" said May.

It sounded more like a question than a statement, but I didn't care because then June repeated it and it sounded like a statement, and a really excited one. Everyone was happy for me. Mom hugged me, and Dad did a way-to-go dance. It was terrible but funny. "You must have gotten your dancing skills from your mother," he joked.

When I was done telling my family, I went to my room and texted Billy. He was really happy for me too. He sent me a text that said "Congratulations" in six different languages, and then he called me and actually said congratulations in six different languages. It made me laugh. I gave Rat a big, happy hug. When I hung up, I called Brynn, but she didn't pick up.

This is going to sound terrible, but I was kind of relieved Brynn didn't answer. I'm not sure what I would have said if she had.

*Friendship is born at that moment
when one person says to another: "What!
You too? I thought I was the only one."*

—*C. S. Lewis*

Tuesday, September 3, 9:32 P.M.
In bed

I can't believe it's 9:30 and I'm already in bed. I'm almost too tired to write, but I have a lot to write about. Today was the first day of dance team practice. After school, I walked a few blocks to the high school with Emily, Kate, and Vanessa. On the way, Kate said her older sister Devon heard some of the older girls were pissed that Ms. Baumann put eighth graders on the team.

"Why would they be mad?" asked Vanessa like she was worried about the reception we might get.

"They didn't seem pissed the other day at tryouts," I said.

Emily smiled and shook her head. "If anything, they're scared we'll be better than they are." She seemed so confident when she said it.

By the time we got to the gym, all the older girls on the team were already there. Ms. Baumann told us to quickly get changed, and then she assigned each one of us a "big sister," one of the high school girls who we're supposed to go to if we need anything. My big sister is a girl named Mady, who's in eleventh grade. Mady's best friend, Bree, is Emily's big sister. Mady and Bree said that since the dance team spends so much time together practicing, we're practically like a dance family. They were really sweet to us. They even gave Emily and me stretchy headbands to wear while we're dancing.

After we were paired with our big sisters, Ms. Baumann talked to us about daily practices and our rehearsal schedule. "We have no time to waste," she said. "Our first competition is at the end of September. Homecoming is in October, and the fall dance show is right before Thanksgiving." She talked for a long time about performances and costumes and the importance of dedication and punctuality. "When you come to practice," she said, "be ready to dance."

She wasn't kidding. We danced for two hours. It was such a hard workout. We did tons of warm-up exercises and stretches and then worked on steps for a hip-hop dance we're going to do in competition.

We learned eight steps at a time and then put those all together before moving on, but Ms. Baumann moved really fast through the steps. It was hard to keep up and remember everything. Anytime anyone messed up, she noticed and told them to pay attention. Emily was standing next to Kate and Vanessa and me, and every time Ms. Baumann let us take a break, Emily would go back over the steps with us to help us remember them.

"I've been dancing since I was four, so I'm used to this," she said. I'm not sure if she was trying to make us feel better or worse, but I didn't care. I was glad to have the extra help.

When practice was over, Emily and I stopped at Smoothie King on the way home. She ordered a Gladiator. "It has the least amount of calories of any smoothie on the menu. As a dancer, you have to watch what you eat," she said.

"I hadn't really thought about that," I said

and ordered a Gladiator too.

"Stick with me," said Emily in her confident way. "I'll give you the crash course on how to be a dancer."

As we were walking home drinking our smoothies, Emily said she was really glad we both made the dance team. "I've wanted to be friends with you for a long time, but it always seemed like you were supertight with Brynn."

I took a long sip of my smoothie. I wasn't sure how to respond. "I am, but I can be friends with other people too," I said.

Emily smiled. "Friends it is," she said.

Even though Emily lives around the corner from me and we've gone to school together our whole lives, we've never been close. It's not like I never wanted to be friends with her, it's just that Emily is pretty and popular and I never thought she wanted to be friends with me. Brynn has always said there's something about Emily she doesn't like. But I like her.

When I got home, Mom wanted to hear all about dance. "Tell me everything!" she said like we were best friends at a sleepover.

I didn't really want to tell her everything. What I wanted to do was call Billy and tell him, so I just told Mom that Ms. Baumann is tough and that being on the dance team will be a lot of hard work.

When I called Billy, I told him most things, but the truth is, there were some things I didn't feel like telling him either. Like about my new stretchy headband or my "big sister" or that I get to perform at the high school homecoming game, because I knew he wouldn't get why those things were important. The person I wanted to tell them to was Brynn. She's the one I always talk to about stuff like that, but I didn't feel like I could talk to her about anything related to dance.

Things have been weird between us since tryouts. All weekend she said she was busy with her parents. Yesterday was Labor Day, so we didn't have school, and today at lunch, she grabbed a yogurt and said she was going to the library to study. Brynn NEVER goes to the library during lunch to study. When I saw her in math, I said, "How did your studying go?"

All she said was, "Huh? Oh yeah, fine." It was like she wasn't even sure what I was talking about, and then she barely spoke to me for the rest of the day.

It feels weird to go to bed without talking to Brynn.

9:47 P.M.

I can't go to bed without talking to Brynn. I'm going to call her, not to talk about dance, but just to call her like I always do. There's nothing weird about that.

9:50 P.M.

I just called Brynn. She didn't pick up. Or answer my text. I'm going to try to go to sleep. Hopefully, things will get less weird very soon. Like tomorrow.

Wednesday, September 4, 5:57 P.M.

Things with Brynn are not less weird. They're more weird.

Today at lunch, Brynn was in the library for the second day in a row, studying and eating yogurt (which is starting to make me wonder if she's suddenly a believer in my Kim Kardashian theory and is hoping to wake up one day with bigger boobs). So I talked to Billy about it. I told him how she doesn't answer my calls or texts and pointed out that she won't even eat lunch with us.

"Brynn is just upset about not making the team," Billy said. "Give her some time and she'll come around."

"I'm not so sure," I told Billy. "It almost seems like she's upset about more than just not making the team, but I'm not sure what it is." I waited to see if Billy would say what I've been thinking, that maybe Brynn likes him for more than just a friend. But Billy just shrugged like he wasn't sure either.

Thursday, September 5, 9:07 P.M.

Brynn didn't eat lunch with me today and neither did Billy. She did her library-and-yogurt thing, and Billy had a student government meeting. When I went into the cafeteria, I got my food and was trying to figure out where to sit when Emily saw me and waved me over to where she was sitting with Kate and Vanessa. "Sit with us," she said.

When I sat down, Emily looked at my tray. "Is that a chicken sandwich?" she asked.

I looked at the other trays on the table. Kate, Vanessa, and Emily all had salads, dressing on the side. I picked up my sandwich and took a bite.

Emily looked at the other salads and held up a forkful of her own. "To keep a dancer's body, I stick to salads for lunch."

Kate and Vanessa looked at me like they were waiting to see what I'd do. Part of me wanted a dancer's body, and part of me wanted to finish my sandwich. "You're right," I said to Emily. Then I got up and got a salad.

Dressing on the side.

Friday, September 6, 10:47 p.m.
At the kitchen table
Drinking hot chocolate
Can't sleep

Three weird things happened today, and I can't stop thinking about any of them.

The first is that Brynn didn't go to the library to study during lunch today. For the first time all week, she ate lunch with Billy and me. I thought it was a sign that maybe things were going back to normal. I tried to show her how happy I was about it.

"Do you want my carrots?" I asked when we sat down at our table with our lunch trays. Brynn loves carrots. When she was little, my mom used to call her Bunny Brynn because she could eat so many.

"I've got my own," she said. She barely even looked at me, then started talking to Billy about an English test they had that afternoon and didn't say another word to me.

The second thing that happened is that the school newspaper came out today. I read it cover to cover, and there wasn't anything in there about the girls who made the dance team. I had a feeling Brynn wouldn't put it on the front page like she'd said she was going to, but I couldn't believe she didn't include it at all. How is it fair that journalists have the power to decide what news is fit to print? That's what I was thinking about when the third weird thing happened today.

Emily and I were walking into the high school gym to go to dance practice, and we saw Matt Parker. He was walking out of gym as we were walking in, and he looked surprised to see me. "California, what are you doing here?" he asked. He smiled his cute, white smile.

Emily's eyes got big. I knew I needed to stay calm. "I made the dance team." I told Matt. "I've been coming over here after school every day for practice."

"Impressive!" He nodded his head for a few seconds. "I had last period PE and stayed to shoot some hoops."

I did the same nod he did, which kind of made it seem like I thought the fact that he stayed to shoot some hoops was impressive too.

Matt laughed. "You're funny, California. I'll see you around," he said. Then he did his head bob thing and left.

"OMG! He's totally into you!" Emily said as soon as he walked away.

"He lives next door to me," I said, like it was no big deal. But I could tell Emily thought it was.

"He called you California!" she said, and I could tell I wasn't the only one who thought my nickname was cute. While we were putting on our dance clothes, Emily kept going on about the fact that Matt was definitely flirting with me. Some of the older girls wanted to know who we were talking about, but I gave Emily a look to keep her mouth shut.

"It was nothing," I whispered.

But Emily just laughed and said it didn't seem like nothing to her.

I'm not sure what it seemed like.

Dance is the hidden language of the soul.

—*Martha Graham*

I'm getting good at writing while I'm in the bathtub. I don't have a choice. My body is so sore from dancing. I've been spending a lot of time here lately, soaking in Epsom salts. Ms. Baumann said they help alleviate muscle ache. I don't even get what they are, but I don't care as long as they work. Every muscle in my body aches.

It's crazy how hard Ms. Baumann makes us work. She's a drill sergeant. Today she reminded us our first competition is in two and a half weeks. "I want the Faraway team ready!" she said. Then she made a long speech about putting our all into our dance. She made us do every step over and over again until everyone got it right.

Still, I feel like I could look a lot better. It's not that I'm not improving. I can tell I am, a little bit, and I think other people can tell too. Today, Mady told me she and Bree think I'm getting better, and one of the ninth graders, Chloe, was really encouraging. "Keep up the good work, April!" she said like she could tell how hard I've been trying to learn the steps.

The problem is I still don't look as good as I'd like to when I dance. Some girls (Emily) seem to have natural dance ability. Some girls (me) have to work hard to get better, but no matter how hard I work, I think I still look like the little girl who used to dance around our living room like a spaz, putting on shows for my parents.

Today, after practice, I actually prayed, "Dear God, could you please make me look naturally graceful and coordinated when I move?" But for some reason, when I said it, I thought about Brynn and instead decided to ask for things to just be normal again between us.

They're still not. We talk if we're both in the same place, like at a table in the cafeteria where it would be totally weird if we didn't talk. But it's only about stuff like school and homework, and I'm the one who does most of the talking. I can tell Brynn wants to say as little to me as possible, and she never says anything about dance. I keep waiting for Brynn to "come around" like Billy said she would, but I'm not so sure it's going to happen.

What I am sure about is that I have to get out of this bathtub soon or May and June are going to get in here with me. They just banged on the door and threatened to do it.

Thursday, September 12, 10:32 P.M.
In bed

I just got off the phone with Billy. I was telling him how hard we've been working on our dances for the competition. I told him there's a hip-hop dance and a jazz dance and the jazz dance is super hard because there are three leaps in it and I suck at doing them. But we hung up because Billy wasn't getting it and I was practically falling asleep (from too much sucky leaping).

Friday, September 13, 5:57 P.M.
In a chair on my patio

Today on the way home from dance I told Emily, "When I leap, my feet leave the ground, but I don't go anywhere. I get no height."

Emily said, "Leaps are really hard." Then she smiled at me like she had a great idea. "Why don't you come to my house tomorrow? I'll show you some tricks that will help."

"That sounds great!" I said. But then I thought about Brynn. I usually go to Brynn's house on the weekends, or she comes to mine, and we hang out. But Brynn didn't say she wanted to hang out this weekend.

If fact, she didn't say anything to me at all.

Sunday, September 15, 12:30 P.M.
At the kitchen table

Last night May had her friend Amelia sleep over. I was sitting on the couch, totally tired but happy from my day with Emily. We worked on leaps for an hour, which was really hard, but then we hung out on her bed eating grapes and reading fashion magazines. She told me she thinks I look good in skinny jeans because I have a small butt. I was thinking about that on the couch when I heard May and Amelia scream and run down the hall.

It was their first sleepover, and Dad had hidden under May's bed, and when they got in bed, he started making really scary growling noises. It was so funny watching them run through the house screaming. It reminded me of the first time Brynn slept over. Dad did the same thing to us, and we ran screaming like idiots just like they did. It made me miss Brynn. I texted her that I had something really funny to tell her.

But she didn't text back.

Wednesday, September 18, 10:17 p.m.

Something kind of weird happened in dance today.

During one of our breaks, I was sitting on the floor of the gym with Emily and Kate and a bunch of the ninth and tenth graders, who were talking about what boys they like.

Darcy, a tenth grader was saying she's into this guy Ben. "He has his license, which totally beats having to have your parents drive you around!" she said. All the older girls were agreeing and talking about how cool it is to go out with guys who drive. I was thinking how cool it was to be sitting there listening to that conversation, which made me start thinking that I feel much older when I'm around my dance friends than I do when I'm with Brynn or even Billy.

Like today at lunch. Billy wanted me to demonstrate a leap for him. "I'm not going to do a leap in the cafeteria!" I said.

Billy laughed. "You better get used to performing in front of people," he said.

I had to explain to him that performing in a competition or a show is completely different from jumping around the cafeteria like a crazy person. I was still thinking about that conversation when I heard someone say Matt Parker's name. It was Chloe.

"We're lab partners in biology, and he's always flirting with me," she said. Then she lowered her voice. "Today, he was whispering some really disgusting things about the frog we were dissecting, and I started laughing so hard, Mr.

Keller sent me to the office! I've never been sent to the office before, but I didn't even care. Matt is so cute," said Chloe.

When she said it, a bunch of the girls agreed. Emily pinched my leg, but I ignored her. I didn't want her to think it made any difference to me if Matt flirts with Chloe or whispers things in her ear that make her laugh hard enough to get sent to the office. And it doesn't. I mean, I have a boyfriend, so why would I care what Matt does?

I don't. Not really. Not at all. OK, maybe I do, just a little.

But I have no idea why.

Thursday, September 19, 9:07 P.M.
In my room
Door locked

Today in dance, some of the older girls were talking about thigh gaps.

"What's a thigh gap?" I asked Mady.

"If you stand with your feet together and look at the space between your thighs, you should have a gap," she said. Then she told me all the best dancers do, particularly ballerinas.

"You don't have to have one, but when you dance it looks better if you do."

When she said that, I looked around to see who had thigh gaps. Mady has one, and so do Bree and Chloe. She has a really big gap. Emily too. Kate doesn't. Vanessa was wearing baggy sweatpants so it was hard to tell if she had one or not. I wanted to look down at my own legs, but I knew it would look really weird if I was looking down at my thighs during dance practice trying to see if I had a gap. So when I came into my room after my bath, I dropped my towel and stood in front of my mirror naked. I stood with my feet together so I could get a good look at my thighs.

When I just stood there, I definitely didn't have a gap. But when I stood up straighter and reached around and pulled back the middle of my thighs, I had a nice gap. I stood in front of my mirror for a long time holding my thighs back and admiring how I looked with a gap. While I was standing there, I couldn't help but wonder if boys would think about me differently if I had a gap, and . . . the boy I was wondering about was Matt. I couldn't help but wonder if he likes Chloe because she has such a big thigh gap. Or if he's kissed her. Or if he remembers kissing me and if he's planning to do it again.

Maybe he's not.

I don't have a thigh gap.

Friday, September 20, 6:53 P.M.
In the den

Since I got home from dance practice, I've been sitting on the couch with May and June watching *SpongeBob* reruns. I'm so tired from dance practice that I'm happy to be sitting on this couch, despite the fact that I'm watching my least favorite show.

On the way home from practice, Emily invited me to come over again tomorrow. "We can practice a little and then hang out and go see a movie or something," she said.

I told her that sounded great. Then Emily linked her arm through mine. "I love that we've gotten to be such good friends! Anything you ever want to tell me you can, like about Matt or whatever."

I was about to open my mouth and remind her that I have a boyfriend so I didn't need to tell her anything about Matt, but Emily looked at me like she got it without me having to say a word. "I know you have a boyfriend, but Matt called you California and he's supercute. That must be tough."

I didn't answer.

"What's up?" asked Emily in a funny voice.

"I'm glad we're friends," I said. And I am. There's stuff I can tell Emily that I could never tell Brynn.

9:08 P.M.
Conflicted!

OMG! Brynn just texted me. I've reread her text like ten times to try and figure out what she means. All it said was "Want to hang out tomorrow? Movie or something?"

I don't know what she means by "or something." Does it mean she just wants to hang out like we always have? Or does she want to talk? It's the first time Brynn has texted me in so long. What if she wants to talk? If I don't do something with her, I know she'll feel like she tried, but I didn't. But I don't see how I can break plans I already made with Emily. I know she'll think she's been really sweet to help me with dance, and she won't like that I'm picking Brynn over her. I have absolutely no idea what to do.

Yes, I do. I'll ask Billy. He's super helpful with this sort of thing.

9:32 P.M.

I just hung up with Billy, and he was no help at all. I was explaining the situation, and before I could even finish, he said, "Go with Brynn."

I don't see how that was even remotely helpful. No matter who I go with, someone will be mad.

*Just because you've got
the emotional range of a teaspoon,
doesn't mean we all have.*

—Hermione Granger

Saturday, September 21, 8:45 P.M.
In my room
My head hurts

I was right that someone would be mad, but that someone was Billy. I just spent the last fifty-eight minutes on the phone with him. I usually love our conversations, but I didn't love this one.

"I don't see how you could have spent the day with Emily and not Brynn," he said.

"How do you even know I spent the day with Emily?" I asked.

That's when Billy said he knew because he spent the day with Brynn, and it was all she could talk about.

I was furious! "I can't believe you and Brynn were talking about me behind my back!"

But Billy didn't seem like he thought he had

to justify why they were doing that. "April, ever since you made the dance team, you've been acting like you've forgotten that Brynn and I are your best friends. She said you never want to hang out with her anymore and that you act like you're better than her because you made the team and she didn't."

I tried to stop him to tell him that wasn't the case at all, but Billy wasn't stoppable. "Brynn said that when you made the team and she didn't, you barely said anything to make her feel better and that you didn't even try to be a good best friend."

I couldn't believe Billy was taking Brynn's side in all this. "I've tried really hard to be a good friend to Brynn." I was practically screaming. "I call her and text her and try to talk to her and be nice to her, but she's been the one ignoring me!"

I gave him a bunch of specific examples, like when I tried to give her my carrots at lunch and she barely even acknowledged me and just started talking to him. "The reason I haven't hung out with her is because she's been acting like she doesn't want to be around me." I was getting more upset with every word. "I *don't* think I'm better than her. I've never said anything like that or even thought it. It's all in her head, not mine."

Billy was quiet, like he was actually listening to what I was saying, so I kept going. "When I made the team and she didn't, the reason I didn't say much to her was because I didn't know what to say. I didn't want to make her feel worse, and it seemed like I was the last person she wanted to talk to about it."

Then I reminded Billy that this wasn't the first time I've talked to him about how Brynn has been acting. "You were the one who said I should be patient and that she would *'come around,'* but she hasn't."

When I was done talking, Billy didn't say anything for a long time. He always thinks about what he's going to say before he says something. I thought he was taking in everything I said and that he was going to say something about how he realized that what Brynn said to him was very one-sided. But that wasn't what he said at all. "April, I get how Brynn feels. Ever since you made the team, you've been spending all your time at practice."

I really didn't think I should have to remind him that dance practice isn't optional. "All I've been telling you since I made the team is how strict and demanding Ms. Baumann is. I shouldn't have to defend myself for something I don't have any control over," I said.

I told Billy that I feel like Brynn is just mad that I made the team and she didn't.

"I understand," said Billy. "But Brynn isn't the only one who misses hanging out with you. I do too."

When he said that, my heart sank in my chest. "Are you mad at me?" I asked Billy.

"At you?" Billy said it like it would be impossible for him to be mad at me. Then he laughed like he'd made a joke.

But to be honest, I couldn't tell if Billy was joking or not.

Sunday, September 22, 5:44 P.M.
Just back from Brynn's

I went over to Brynn's house to talk to her. I

didn't even call her to tell her I was coming over. I just went. When she opened the door, I said, "We need to talk." And she was like, "Yeah, we do."

So we sat down on the floor of her room and talked for a really long time. Even though I was the one who went to talk to Brynn, she was the one who did most of the talking.

"April, ever since you made the dance team, I feel like you haven't been a good friend to me." She repeated a lot of the stuff Billy had said on the phone.

I tried to explain to her that I've tried to be a good friend and that she's the one who has been avoiding me. At first, she acted like she had no idea what I was talking about, so I gave her lots of the same examples that I gave Billy. I could tell by the way she sat up straight and crossed her arms across her chest while I was talking that she didn't like me pointing out what she had done. That's when she cut me off. "April, I tried to get together with you yesterday, and it hurt that you chose to hang out with Emily over me. I thought you would have known that I wanted to get together so we could talk and work everything out," she said.

"I told you, I'd already made plans with Emily, and I didn't feel like I could just break them," I said. Then I reminded Brynn that I texted her and asked her if she wanted to do something today, since I was already doing something on Saturday, and she never even responded to that text.

But Brynn ignored that. "Why do you want to be friends with Emily?" she asked me without waiting for an answer. "I've never really liked Emily. I don't trust her, and I don't think you should either."

I didn't see why it was any of Brynn's business if I want to be friends with Emily. "She's just my dance friend," I said.

That seemed to make Brynn feel a little better. Then she said the reason she couldn't respond when she got my text was that she was hurt. Part of me felt badly, but another part of me wanted to tell her that I was hurt too, that I didn't like how instead of texting me back and making a plan to talk on Sunday, she decided to talk to Billy about me. But when I looked at her and was about to say that, she really did look upset, so instead I said, "This is all so dumb. As much as I like being on the dance team, I would like it so much more if you had made it too." And even though I wasn't sure I wanted to say it, I told her that I was sorry I hadn't been a better friend.

The look on Brynn's face changed when I said that. She leaned over and gave me a big hug. "April, of course, I forgive you."

I didn't really think I was the only one that needed to be forgiven, but Brynn changed the subject and told me her mom said she could have a party on Halloween since she never got to have a real birthday party when she turned thirteen. She said her mom thought turning thirteen was a huge deal, so she could have a BIG party at her house with a DJ. "We should stop talking about all this other nonsense when we have a party to plan!"

So we stopped talking about "nonsense" and started talking about music and costumes and food and decorations. I could tell she was relieved. To be honest, I was too. Brynn's my best friend, but some days, she's not the easiest person to talk to. Like today. But her party is going to be awesome, and I'm already thinking about my costume.

I can't wait!

11:07 p.m.
Can't sleep

I keep thinking about my conversation today with Brynn. I'm glad we talked, but one thing still bothers me. Why did Brynn have to talk to Billy about me behind my back?

At the end of seventh grade, when I kissed Matt, she said she didn't see how I could kiss Matt after Billy had kissed me and that Billy is the cutest guy in our grade and that any girl would want him as her boyfriend. It made me think *she* would want that, but then she didn't act like she did, so I stopped thinking it.

But now, I'm thinking it again. I can't help it. I think about her calling Billy to come over and watch us dance and how she danced right in front of him. I think about her hanging out with him all day yesterday and talking about me.

I should be fine with them hanging out, right? Billy and Brynn and I have all been best friends since third grade, and I know they've done stuff together in the past without me. But I don't like that they did stuff without me yesterday.

The truth is . . . I don't like it at all.

10:32 P.M.

I just called Billy and told him I'm sorry I haven't been around more lately. "I miss spending time with you. Maybe we can do something fun together next weekend?" I said.

Billy seemed to like hearing that. "It's a date," he said.

It was such a Billy thing to say.

Clear and sweet is my soul,
And clear and sweet is
all that is not my soul.

—*Walt Whitman*, *"Song of Myself"*

Monday, September 23, 9:45 P.M.
In my room

Our costumes came in for the dance competition, and Ms. Baumann had us try them on this afternoon to make sure we all had the right sizes. They were tank leotards in red or white, which are our school colors, and matching tights. My costume was all white, and when I put it on, the first thing I noticed was how small my boobs looked compared to lots of the older girls. I looked like a kid they would get paid to babysit.

"Do you think I should wear a padded bra with my leotard? I asked Mady.

She shook her head like that wasn't a good idea. "Ms. Baumann is really strict about straps showing," she said.

"Stick your boobs out," said Emily, who

obviously overheard what I had asked Mady. When she said it, she stood up super straight and stuck out her chest, which is much bigger than mine, like she was demonstrating what she meant.

Everyone laughed. It was pretty funny the way she did it. Even though she was kind of making fun of me, I laughed too. For some reason, I didn't really mind. I guess I was happy to be part of the group that was laughing.

Thursday, September 26, 10:07 P.M.

Billy just called to remind me about our "date" on Saturday.

"I have the dance competition on Saturday, so we have to go Sunday," I said. I couldn't believe I had to remind him, since the competition is pretty much the only thing I've been talking about lately.

But Billy said he didn't realize the competition was this Saturday, and he seemed kind of annoyed that we had to go on our date on Sunday instead.

So I changed the subject. "Rat wants to know what the President of Faraway Middle

School thinks about the new bench tables in the cafeteria."

Billy's mood seemed to change when I said that. "Tell Rat they're too hard and they give me a sore butt," he said. Then he laughed.

Saturday, September 28, 6:54 P.M.
In the tub (where I will be for the foreseeable future)

I'm almost too tired (and definitely too sore) to write much, but I have to.

Today was such a good day. The competition was this morning, and it was amazing. When I woke up, I wasn't sure it was going to be. I was a wreck. My hands were shaking so much I couldn't even put my hair up the right way. Mom had to do it for me.

But when I got to the auditorium and everyone on the team was helping each other put the finishing touches on our makeup, I started to get more excited than scared. Ms. Baumann gave us a really nice pep talk about how we were all ready, and the older girls on the team were really sweet and reassuring.

Walking onstage for our first dance was terrifying. But once the music started, I focused on each step, and before I knew it, we were done. The second dance seemed a little easier. While we were waiting for the results to be announced, I felt like such a part of the team. Everyone was complimenting each other on our performance. Mady told me I danced great and that she was really proud of me.

The best news is that we came in second place in jazz and first place in hip-hop! When our first-place win was announced, Ms. Baumann was all smiles. I'm not even sure I'd ever even seen her smile before that. We went up onstage as a team to get our trophy, and afterward, the whole team was hugging. It was like a scene in a movie that the director would have to shoot a bunch of times to get just right, but in this case, it was perfect without even trying.

Sunday, September 29, 4:45 P.M.
Just back from my date with Billy

Today was my first real date, so I had no idea what to expect. Billy called this morning and told me to get ready to go on a bike ride. Honestly, my legs were so sore from extra practices this week that going on a bike ride was the last thing I wanted to do, but I didn't tell Billy that.

"We're going to ride to Oak Lake Park," Billy said when he came to get me. I must have made a face like I wasn't up for that ride, which is really long, because Billy just laughed.

"I have some surprises for you, April Sinclair," he said. Billy knows how much I love surprises, so even though I didn't want to go on a long bike ride, I was excited to see what he had.

When we got to the park, we rode our bikes around the lake until we got to this hidden-away area with a bunch of huge rocks. We left our bikes against some trees, and Billy adjusted his backpack, which was pretty full, on his back.

"What's in there?" I asked him in a teasing way. But all Billy would say was that I would find out soon enough.

Billy took my hand, and we walked across the rocks. It was cool because the rocks were big enough that they actually stuck out above the water and formed a line that led out into the lake.

It was kind of like walking on water. We walked out to the farthest rock, which was mostly flat, and sat down on top of it. It was just Billy and me, surrounded by the waters of Oak Lake, a few stray ducks, and some chirping birds. (That sounds kind of weirdly poetic, but it was actually nice.)

"Picnic time!" Billy said when we sat down. He brought out cheese and crackers, grapes and strawberries, turkey sandwiches, and two bottles of lemonade. It was so cute. We ate our lunch sitting next to each other on the rocks. When we were done, we threw the leftover bits of our sandwiches to the ducks on the lake. Then Billy brought out a piece of cake on a plate and two forks. "It's a little smushed from being in my backpack," he said.

I didn't care. It still tasted good.

After we ate the cake, Billy said he had a real surprise for me. He took a little box out of his backpack. It was wrapped in the comics section from the Sunday paper, and it had a pink bow around it. It looked so cute. "I like your wrap job," I told Billy.

He smiled. "I hope you like what's inside too." He handed me the box.

I opened it slowly. Inside was a black cord bracelet with a little pink glass heart on it. My heart started beating faster when I saw it. The bracelet was just the right mix of sweet and tough. "I love it," I said the moment I saw it.

Billy slid the bracelet out of the box and tied it around my wrist. I held my wrist up so we could both see it. Then something happened that I hadn't expected.

Billy picked up my hand and kissed my wrist right where the heart fell.

We were on a date, so I thought he would kiss me, just not on my wrist. He's kissed me lots of times before, but always on my cheek or my lips. It felt kind of weird to be kissed on my wrist. I guess I made a face like I didn't like it.

Billy was quiet for a minute. It was kind of awkward. "What are you thinking?" he asked.

I didn't want to say what I was really thinking, which was that it seemed weird to kiss my wrist or that I hoped it didn't taste salty from riding my bike so far and sweating like a pig.

Instead, what I said was that I thought it was really sweet that he gave me such a nice gift.

The bracelet felt all right, but to be honest, something about the kiss on the wrist felt wrong.

There's no place like home.

—*Dorothy, The Wizard of Oz*

Ms. Baumann might have been happy when we won the competition on Saturday, but today she was all business when she went through the homecoming schedule.

"Homecoming is October 18—that gives us less than three weeks to prepare!" She said it like three weeks was the same thing as three days. Then she talked about the dance we'll be doing at the pep rally that Friday and the routine we'll be performing during halftime of the game on Saturday.

When she was done, some of the girls started cheering like they were showing their school spirit a little early, but Ms. Baumann stopped them and said there would be time to cheer later. She called out Emily, Vanessa, Kate, and me. "Girls, you will be given permission to leave the middle school for the pep rally. As we get closer, we'll coordinate your schedules." Emily and I high-fived. Then Ms. Baumann told us to get ready to work on our dances for both performances, and that's what we did.

When I got home, I called Billy. I was excited to tell him about performing at the homecoming game and the pep rally. "You can come to the game and see us dance!" I said.

"That's cool," Billy said, but I kind of got the feeling he didn't really share my enthusiasm.

Saturday, October 5, 12:32 P.M.
On my bed, too tired to move

I haven't written anything all week because I haven't had time. All I've done is wake up, go to school, go to dance practice, come home, do my homework, and go to bed. Ms. Baumann has made our practices even longer than usual so that we're ready in time for homecoming. All we do is go over and over and over our dances.

If someone gave Ms. Baumann a page in the

yearbook, her quote would read: "Take it from the top."

Sunday, October 6, 4:45 P.M.
In my bathroom
Trying to wash makeup off my face
Not sure it's washable

I called Brynn, Billy, and Emily today to see if they wanted to do something, but they were all busy so I let May and June play beauty shop on me.

BIG MISTAKE.

Tuesday, October 8, 1:47 P.M.
My body, in study hall
My brain, somewhere else

Before study hall, Brynn invited me over after dance practice. "I want you to see my Halloween costume before I order it," she said.

"Sounds like fun," I told her, and it does. I have a test next period in social studies that I should be studying for, but who can think about the three branches of the American government with Halloween around the corner?

Going to Brynn's house to help her order her costume was a lot less fun than I thought it would be. In fact, it was pretty annoying. When I got there, Brynn said, "I'm going to be Dorothy from *The Wizard of Oz*." Then she showed me the costume and all the accessories down to the ruby slippers she was planning to order.

"Wow! That's a supercute costume," I said. Then I told Brynn that I'm coming as a flapper girl. "Mom is making a really cute minidress with fringe on it for me. She said I can order some gloves and a headpiece and some fake pearls to go with it."

Brynn frowned. "Actually, I was thinking that we could both go as characters from *The Wizard of Oz*. You can either be the Scarecrow or the Tin Man. I'm going to talk to Heather and see if she wants to be whichever one you don't want to be, and Billy can be the Lion."

I didn't want to dress up as a scarecrow or a tin man. "Mom has already started on my costume," I told Brynn. But that didn't seem to make any difference to her.

"You can save it for another time." She shrugged like it was really no big deal. Then, when I didn't say anything for a few seconds, she crossed her arms across her chest and looked at me. "April, I think it would be really fun to all wear costumes from *The Wizard of Oz*." She bent down and scooped up her dog, Riley, and held him up in front of me. "Riley can be Toto," she said like it was all decided.

I couldn't believe what I was hearing. Just because it's Brynn's party doesn't mean she can decide what people are wearing. It's really babyish, in my opinion, to all wear *Wizard of Oz* costumes. Plus, I already have a cute flapper costume.

Brynn tapped her foot like she was waiting for my answer, so I just said, "Whatever."

Wednesday, October 9, 8:45 p.m.

After practice today, Emily and I walked home together. She said there was a cute store just off our route that she went to with her mom and her little sister yesterday, and there was something in the store she wanted to show me. When we got there, she had two matching Dance On graphic tees on hold behind the counter. "One is for you, and one is for me!" she said.

We tried them on, and they were supercute. "When I saw these, I knew we had to have them, so I got my mom to buy them yesterday!" she said.

"I love it!" I said.

"I'm so glad!" said Emily. Then she hugged me and said, "April, you're like my new best friend."

For some reason, it made me really happy when she said that.

Friday, October 11, 10:15 P.M.
Just home from the diner

Tonight was one of the most annoying nights ever.

I went to the diner with my family to celebrate my parent's fifteenth anniversary. (I personally find it hard to imagine how they've put up with each other for fifteen years. I've only been putting up with them for thirteen, and it has definitely been a challenge.)

Dad closed early and planned a surprise celebration for Mom. He invited everyone we know and love (his words, not mine)—Gaga; all of my aunts, uncles, and cousins on my mom's side; my dad's brother, Uncle Martin; his son Sam; some of our neighbors; and Billy and Brynn and their families.

Dad went all out. He blew up giant pictures of himself and mom from their wedding and hung them up everywhere. The pictures were old and grainy, and their clothes and hair looked so ridiculous.

Dad cooked all the same foods he and Mom served at their wedding, and he even made a special vanilla cream pie that he said resembled their wedding cake. I didn't think so from the pictures, but Mom seemed touched by his gesture.

After Dad served dinner, he made a toast to Mom, and then he sang a song he wrote for her. He has a horrible voice. Mom actually cried. I don't know why. Maybe her ears hurt.

I honestly thought the whole thing was ridiculous and embarrassing.

When Dad was done singing, Gaga walked over to me and said, "April, why the sour look?"

I thought the answer to that question was pretty obvious.

Saturday, October 12, 12:45 P.M.

This morning at dance, after we finished practicing our dances for the pep rally and the halftime show, Ms. Baumann gave out the T-shirts we're going to be wearing for home-coming. They're supercute red fitted shirts with the school logo on them, and she said we should all wear them with denim shorts.

"You can wear a padded bra with this one," Mady whispered in my ear.

I smiled at her. I'm definitely going to.

5:44 P.M.
Sitting on my bed
Billy just left

When I got home from dance, I invited Billy over. I haven't seen him for a while because I've been so busy with dance, but Mom was making homemade pizzas for lunch, and I know he loves pizza. When he walked into the kitchen, May and June were putting toppings on their pizzas. When they saw Billy, they got super excited.

"You can be my pizza decorator," said May.

"Yeah, you can be mine too," said June.

My sisters love Billy. Anyway, there were three small pizzas, and Billy spelled out May with pepperoni on one and June with black olives on another. Then he looked at me. "Can I be your pizza decorator too?" he asked.

"Sure," I said. I would've rather just put toppings on like a normal pizza, but Billy seemed like he was enjoying playing it up for May and June.

He spelled out my name in mushrooms and basil, and then he made me hold it up while he took a picture of me with his phone. He actually made it his new phone wallpaper, which kind of annoyed me. It wasn't even a good picture of me.

After we all ate our pizzas, Mom and Dad went outside to work in the yard and May and June went with them. Billy and I sat down on the couch to watch TV. I turned it on and sat there without saying anything. I don't even know what we were watching.

"You're really quiet," Billy said after a few minutes.

I knew I was being grumpy, but I couldn't help it. Decorating pizzas with Billy seemed so childish and stupid. I felt the same way about it that I did about Brynn wanting to wear matching Halloween costumes or my dad singing an off-key love song to my mom in front of everyone we know. I feel so different when I'm around the girls on the dance team and Emily than when I'm around Billy or Brynn or my family.

I was thinking about that when Billy poked me in the ribs. "Earth to April," he said like he was waiting for an answer.

I don't know why I said what I did next, but I told Billy about thigh gaps and that I don't have one.

He started laughing. "I like you the way you are," he said.

For some reason, that annoyed me even more.

So many roads. So many detours. So many choices. So many mistakes.

—Carrie Bradshaw

How can life be just fine one minute and a disaster the next? I don't know if anyone else's life is like that, but mine is. I can't believe what happened tonight. I almost don't want to write about it.

After dinner, I took Gilligan on a walk and I saw Matt. He wasn't walking his dog. He was just outside. When he saw me, he started walking with me.

"How's dance team going?" he asked. He was being really friendly, asking me about the team and what we're doing.

I wasn't feeling weird around him like I usually do. I was just in a good mood. I was actually feeling kind of cute and chatty. "I think there's a girl on the team who likes you," I said.

Matt smiled. "Really? Who?"

But I wouldn't tell him. He kept asking, but I just kept shaking my head like I wasn't going to say anything. "C'mon, April," he said like he really wanted to coax it out of me.

I ran my fingers across my lips like they were zipped shut.

Matt laughed. "Well, it just so happens that there's a girl on the team that I like. Can you guess who it is?" he asked.

I kind of had a feeling we were talking about the same person. "Chloe?" I said.

Matt frowned. "Why would you think I like Chloe?" he asked.

I wasn't completely sure what to say at that point, but I told him what Chloe said about how he flirts with her in bio and how he made her laugh so hard she got sent to the office.

Matt shook his head. "I don't like Chloe," he said.

"It seems like you do," I said back.

Matt looked at me in a weird way, like he thought I was challenging him. "I don't like

Chloe." His voice was lower this time. He stopped walking, so I stopped too. We were standing next to a tree in Dr. Black's yard. It was dark outside, but I could feel Matt looking down at me. Then he whispered in my ear, "I like you, California."

He stood there for what felt like a long time, his eyes looking into mine. I tried to look away, but I couldn't. Then Matt pulled me in next to him and kissed me.

I wasn't expecting him to do that. Everything in my brain started to swirl together. It wasn't just that he kissed me. It was the way he kissed me.

Matt's fingers dug into my waist. His mouth was pressed hard against mine. Then I could feel his hands moving down my back. His fingers were grazing the top of my butt, pulling me in even closer to him. I arched my back and pulled in my stomach.

He pulled his lips away from mine. "You have an amazing body," he whispered.

I couldn't believe he'd said that. I'm not sure I believed it, but I wanted to. I silently thanked

Emily for all her diet advice.

Matt's lips were back on mine. I leaned into him. It was like my body was my body, but my brain belonged to someone else. No one had ever taught me to do what I was doing, but somehow instinctively, I seemed to know.

I felt the tip of Matt's tongue against my lips, daring me to open them. Gilligan pulled on his leash. Part of me knew I should break away, but I didn't. It was like my brain was telling me to stop, but the rest of me wanted to know what his tongue would feel like.

I parted my lips, just a little. When I did, Matt's tongue slipped into my mouth. The warmth and the pressure of it against mine scared me and I pulled back.

The magical spell was broken. What was I doing? I ran the back of my hand along my mouth. I wanted to wipe away what just happened. "You shouldn't have done that," I said.

Matt looked at me. "Really? Why?"

My good mood from earlier evaporated. I didn't know what to say. I didn't want to be standing next to a tree in Dr. Black's yard with

Matt Parker looking down at me waiting for a response. Thoughts of Billy flooded my brain. "I have a boyfriend," I whispered.

Matt looked at me in his confident I-have-an-answer-for-everything way. "Then this will be our secret," was the last thing he said before I turned and walked home with Gilligan.

11:53 P.M.

I'll never be able to fall asleep. I feel so awful. I can't believe what happened tonight. How could I kiss Matt?

I keep thinking about Billy. So what that I was annoyed with him this afternoon or that I thought the wrist kiss on our date was a little weird. Billy is sweet and smart and adorable. Why in the world would I kiss Matt when I have such an amazing boyfriend? And why would I let him kiss me the way I did? I feel sick.

Matt's words keep rattling around inside my head. *This will be our secret.*

I don't want to have a secret with Matt Parker.

I know Matt said he likes me, but . . . does he really like me? And do I like Matt? I hardly know him, but I like the way he kisses me. Is that terrible to say? I like Billy, but it doesn't feel the same when he kisses me.

My mind keeps going back over every millisecond of my kiss with Matt.

How can I wish I hadn't kissed Matt when I can't stop thinking about it? What's wrong with me? I'm so confused. How could I do this to Billy? Why am I even still thinking about Matt? I don't want to be thinking about him. Does it make me a bad person that I am?

All I know for sure is that Matt messes up my life. That's the problem with him. It's what happened when he kissed me at the end of seventh grade, and now, it's happening all over again. He's like a curse. I just want to go to sleep and stop thinking about any of this. Hopefully, when I wake up, I'll find out this whole thing was just a bad dream.

But it feels more like a real-life nightmare.

Your secrets are safe with me,
Loretta . . . I'm not listening.

—*The Lockhorns*

Sunday, October 13, 8:32 A.M.
Still in bed

Last night was definitely not a dream. I wish there was a way I could make it unhappen. I'd like to go back in time and do things differently. There were so many things I could have done instead of taking Gilligan for a walk. I could have washed my hair or painted my nails or watched *SpongeBob* with May and June. It wasn't like anyone even asked me to walk Gilligan—I just did it, and I really wish I hadn't. My brain was so clear before I kissed Matt, and now it's all cloudy.

I need to take a deep breath and relax. I can't go back in time and change anything, but maybe I can pretend like it never happened, and it will be almost like it didn't.

10:07 A.M.
In the kitchen
No appetite

When I went into the kitchen, Mom asked me if I'd like pancakes. "No thanks," I told her. I picked up a banana, hoping that she'd leave me alone, but she didn't.

"April, are you eating properly? Are you not eating pancakes because of dance?" She asked the second question before I could even answer the first.

We'd already had one talk about my new eating habits, and Mom didn't like that I wasn't eating some of the foods I used to eat all the time.

"I'm just not in the mood for pancakes," I told Mom. I wish it was only because of dance.

11:02 A.M.

Trying to pretend like last night never happened isn't working. My brain is stuck on kissing Matt. Why am I still thinking about this? I need to stop. I'm glad I have homework to do. Hopefully, if I think about rational numbers, I'll stop thinking about kissing Matt. That sounds rational, doesn't it?

1:17 P.M.
At my desk

I can't think about anything but last night. I've even tried using the Mosquito Technique. I learned it at camp. If you think about the mosquitoes, they drive you crazy. But if you relax and pretend like you don't even know they're there, it's almost like they're not.

1:20 P.M.

Apparently, this technique only works with mosquitoes.

Monday, October 14, 1:27 P.M.
Study hall

Life at Faraway Middle School is going on around me. Kids are changing classes, taking tests, playing sports, and eating bad cafeteria food. I'm doing all those thing too, but I'm also trying to avoid Billy (which I've managed to do so far today, but only because I purposely picked a scab off my knee and went to the nurses' office during lunch to get a Band-Aid).

I'm also living with a secret, and I can't stand it. I could hardly concentrate in my classes. I really, really wish I could talk to Brynn. She's my oldest friend, and I need her advice. I thought about talking to her this morning during break, but I decided not to. As much as I'd like to, I know she wouldn't understand.

I can just hear what she'd say. *"April, you shouldn't have kissed Matt the first time, and I can't imagine why you did a second time!"* Then she'd say that she kept it from Billy the last time I kissed Matt, but she doesn't want to do it again. She'd give me her speech about how we're all friends, and if he was going out with any other girl who kissed someone else and she found out, she'd tell him.

But the main reason I can't tell her is that I think she might be happy, because it would mean Billy and I are over and he'd be free for other girls. Like her.

I can't believe I just wrote that.

Not all of me thinks it, but part of me keeps going back over the day at Brynn's house when she called Billy to come over and watch us dance. She was so excited to dance in front of him. Then she went behind my back and talked to him about how I wasn't being a good friend. As much as I want to talk to somebody about this and figure out what to do, I know Brynn isn't that somebody.

10:07 P.M.
In bed

I hardly saw Billy at school today, luckily, and he couldn't talk long on the phone tonight because he has a big math test tomorrow. I was worried I would see Matt when I went to the gym for dance practice. But I didn't.

One day down, the rest of my life to go.

Tuesday, October 15, 8:22 P.M.

I saw Billy today at lunch, and he said, "April, duty calls. As president of the student body I must attend a mandatory meeting, which means I can't eat lunch with you." Then he actually gave me a quick peck on the cheek and said, "Sorry I'm being a bad boyfriend."

I couldn't believe those words came out of his mouth. I know he was trying to be funny and sweet, but it was the one thing he could have said that actually made me feel worse.

Somehow, I did manage to avoid Matt when I went to dance practice.

Hooray for small victories.

Wednesday, October 16, 10:02 P.M.
In bed

Keeping other people's secrets is hard, but keeping your own is even harder. It has been five days since Matt and I kissed. I thought maybe I'd be able to just forget it happened, but it's the only thing I can think about.

During practice today, Ms. Baumann actually called me out. "April, the pep rally is on Friday. Everyone looks ready but you."

It was mortifying. Everyone was looking at me. I actually felt like there were little thought bubbles over my head and everybody could see what I'd been thinking about.

On the way home from practice, Emily said, "April, you haven't been yourself all week. Is everything OK?"

"I'm having my period," I lied.

Emily looked at me in a sweet way, like she meant what she was about to say. "You know you can tell me if something is bothering you."

I nodded.

"We're best friends," said Emily. "And that's what best friends are for."

When she said that, part of me really wanted to tell her what happened. But part of me still wasn't sure if it was a good idea.

10:37 P.M.

Billy called tonight, and we talked for twenty-three minutes, which is short for us. Our conversation sounded normal, I think. The only thing that was different was me.

I feel so terrible about what I did. I don't know how I could have done what I did to Billy. I really don't. Dad just came in my room and told me to turn off my light and go to sleep. When he kissed me good night, he told me he was proud of me.

For what? Seriously.

Emily, Kate, Vanessa, and I got to leave school after third period to go to the high school for the pep rally. It should have been such an exciting day, but my head was such a mess.

When we got to the gym, all the older girls were already in the bathroom changing. "Girls, get in your costumes quickly," Ms. Baumann said to all of us. "The pep rally is starting in five minutes." We all changed, and just as we were going into the gym, I had a terrible stomach ache.

"I have to go to the bathroom," I told Ms. Baumann.

She pointed to Emily. "Stay with her!" she said, like I needed a buddy. Then she looked at me and told me to hurry. She obviously had no patience for stomach aches.

When I finished, Emily and I were on our way to the gym to join the rest of the dance team, and as we were walking, we saw Matt Parker.

He came over to us and put his hand on my arm and stopped me like he wanted to say something. I think he was actually looking at my chest. I would have given anything not to have been wearing the padded bra that I'd begged Mom to buy for me.

"You look cute," said Matt. He smiled at me.

Emily's eyes shot up.

"Thanks," I said. It was the first time we'd talked since we kissed. It felt so awkward to be standing there next to him with Emily watching. "I have to go," I said. I didn't even care if it sounded like all I do is use the bathroom.

I grabbed Emily's arm, and we hurried over to where the rest of the team was waiting. I knew she wanted to say something about what happened, but fortunately, there was no time.

The pep rally was starting. Everyone in the gym was screaming. "GO!" yelled Ms. Baumann when it was our turn to dance. We ran out to the floor of the gym and took our places. The music started. Somehow, I don't know how, I made it through the dance without messing up.

On the way back to the bathroom afterward, Emily stopped me. "What's the deal with Matt?" She stood in front of me like she was waiting for an answer. But I didn't give her one.

This was supposed to be a pep rally, not a tell-all.

Saturday, October 19, 10:02 P.M.
Homecoming

I told Emily what happened. I hadn't planned to tell her, but it all came tumbling out before our halftime performance tonight. I was a wreck during the whole first half. Billy was there. Matt was there. All I wanted to do was avoid both of them. Even though I knew they knew where the dance team was sitting, I literally was slumped down in my chair like I was trying to hide.

"What's wrong with you?" Emily asked.

"Nothing," I said. Even I knew my voice didn't sound normal. All I wanted to do was get through the dance we had to do at halftime, but I was a fidgeting mess. As the countdown to halftime neared, I couldn't sit still.

Emily kept looking at me. "I think I know what's going on," she said with two minutes to go before halftime. She gave me this look like she already knew something scandalous had happened. And that's when it all came pouring out. I couldn't hold it in any longer.

I told her everything. How Matt pulled me into him and kissed me, then French kissed me.

I told her I was upset and wished I hadn't kissed him and that when I reminded Matt that I had a boyfriend, the only thing he had to say was that it would be our secret.

When I finished, Emily wrapped her arm around me. "You poor thing, you must have been dying holding it in for so long. You should have told me sooner!"

I told her it was really hard to keep that secret and that I've been feeling terrible about what I did to Billy but that it felt good to tell someone.

"Don't worry," said Emily. "Your secrets are safe with me."

Then Ms. Baumann said to get in line, and before I knew it, we were on the field in front of thousands of screaming Faraway football fans. We did the dance we'd been practicing for weeks, without one misstep. When we finished, we ran off the field to everyone clapping and cheering. "Great job, girls!" said Ms. Baumann.

But I didn't feel great. I was happy that the performance went well, and right before the performance, it felt pretty good to talk to Emily and get everything off my chest. But after we finished dancing, I started to feel like it was a bad idea to tell Emily what happened with Matt. I pulled Emily aside and reminded her that she said my secrets were safe with her. She nodded like they were.

But I had a gnawing feeling that they might not be.

11:32 P.M.
Starting to panic

I'm not so sure my secrets are safe with Emily. What Brynn said about not trusting her keeps running through my head. I texted Emily an hour ago to remind her not to tell anybody about what I told her, and she never texted me back. Crap. What have I done, and is there any way to undo it?

Dear God, please don't let it be a bad idea that I told Emily.

> *A lie gets halfway around the world before the truth has time to get its pants on.*
>
> —*Winston Churchill*

Monday, October 21, 5:52 P.M.
I've said it before
This time I mean it
Worst day of my life
Officially

Everything at school today seemed fine.

I played volleyball in PE. I took a test in math. I ate a salad, no dressing for lunch. My problems started at dance. Actually, they started on the way to dance. I always walk to the high school with Emily, Kate, and Vanessa. Today I waited by the front gate for them, where I always do, but they never showed up.

I thought maybe they were running late, so I texted Emily, but she didn't answer.

I had to leave. We get in so much trouble with Ms. Baumann if we're late. But as I walked to the high school, I had a terrible feeling that being late was the least of my problems.

I knew I was right the minute I walked into the gym. When I got there, Emily, Kate, and Vanessa were already there, and they were sitting on the opposite side of the gym talking to all the ninth-grade girls on the team. They were all huddled together like they were discussing something serious.

My stomach was in knots. I didn't know if I should go over to where they were, but I felt like it would seem weird if I didn't. When I got to them, everyone stopped talking and looked at me.

The gym was too quiet. Chloe broke the silence. "April, how could you?" she asked. "I told you Matt and I are a thing." I didn't know what to say. I looked at Emily. Who had she told my secret to? What had she said? She wouldn't even look at me.

Then everyone started talking like I wasn't standing there. They were all saying all kinds of stuff, and not just what I told Emily, which was that I'd kissed Matt and wished I hadn't.

She's secretly going out with Matt.

They live next door to each other so it has been easy to keep it a secret.

I've seen them talking in the gym all the time.

I have a feeling it has been going on for a long time.

Their words swirled around me. I just stood there. I didn't know what else to do. Every time someone said something, they'd all look at me like I was supposed to defend myself or confirm if it was true or not.

I couldn't speak. My brain was incapable of forming words. I couldn't believe what I was listening to. I don't know how the story got so out of hand. I felt like I was going to throw up or cry or both. Ms. Baumann came in then, and we started practice.

"April, please try to keep up," she said two different times.

But I couldn't. It was my worst rehearsal ever. And not just because I kept messing up. No one wanted to be near me. The girls in my dancing line kept scooting away from me, and when we did the partners part of the dance, Amy, who was supposed to put her arm around my waist, wouldn't even touch me. When practice was over, Emily left the gym right away with Vanessa and Kate. She didn't wait for me. Not that I would have wanted her to.

I can't believe Emily told everyone. I thought I could trust her. I thought we were friends. She said my secrets were safe with her, but clearly, they weren't.

Brynn was right. She usually is. And now everyone on the dance team knows what happened, or what they think happened. I feel sick. Can my life get any worse? I doubt it.

8:46 P.M.
In my room
On my bed
Heartsick

I thought wrong. Things got so much worse.

I was so upset about everyone on the dance team being mad at me, I hadn't even thought about how other people would react.

Brynn just called me. She heard what happened, and she's furious. Furious that I kissed

Matt, furious that I told other people and didn't tell her, and furious that I would do this to Billy.

"I'm sure half of what you heard isn't even true," I said.

"If half was true, it's bad enough," Brynn said back.

I started crying. It was bad enough that Brynn was mad. "What am I going to do if Billy finds out?" I asked her. Brynn was quiet for a minute. Then she said three of the scariest words I've ever heard.

"He already knows."

Dogs never bite me. Just humans.

—*Marilyn Monroe*

Tuesday, October 22, 9:07 P.M.

Today was the first school day since third grade that I didn't speak to Billy or Brynn. Neither of them was in the cafeteria at lunch. I actually never even saw Billy. When I saw Brynn in study hall, she looked down at the book on her desk like she was studying, and in math, we had a test, so I couldn't talk to her.

The same thing happened with the girls on the dance team.

There are no words to describe how I feel.

Wednesday, October 23, 5:52 P.M.
Just home from dance practice

I don't want to be on the dance team anymore. I know I can't quit, but I wish I could. Today, Emily, Kate, and Vanessa walked to the high school without me (again).

At practice, everyone was crowding around Chloe like they had to protect her from me. The other girls were doing everything possible to make me feel like I wasn't wanted there. They weren't looking at me or talking to me or even dancing near me when they were supposed to be.

During the break, I pulled Emily aside. I knew it probably wasn't the place to do it, but I had to talk to her and I didn't know where else she would talk to me.

"What did you say to everyone?" I asked her.

She gave me this weird, blank look. "I have no idea what you're talking about."

I couldn't believe her. "Emily, you're the only one I told, and now everyone knows. You said my secrets were safe with you."

Emily's mouth dropped open like she was shocked by what I was saying. "I can't believe you're accusing me of telling people your secret," she said. She crossed her arms across her chest like she was getting more upset by the second. "For your information, when I got to dance yesterday, everyone was already talking about it."

She paused. "Maybe your boyfriend was the one who told people."

I wanted to believe she was talking about Billy, but I knew she meant Matt. I felt like I'd been punched in the gut. "I don't know why you'd call Matt my boyfriend," I said. "And I don't think he told anyone."

Emily shook her head like it was sad that I couldn't see the truth. Then Ms. Baumann said break was over and to get back into formation.

I made it through the rest of practice, but I don't know how. I'm a pariah. That was one of our vocab words in English. At first, I had to look it up to see what it meant, but now I know firsthand. I'm a snake in the henhouse. A fly at a barbecue. A seagull at a beach picnic. Nobody on the team wants me there.

We're on the same page as far as that goes. I don't want to be there either.

Friday, October 25, 9:47 p.m.
Heartbroken

Billy hadn't called or texted or spoken to me all week, so when I came home from dance practice, I decided to walk Gilligan over to his house and go talk to him. At first, I thought our talk was going well because right when I got to his house, he told me he was actually about to come over to my house because he wanted to talk to me too. We sat down on the steps of his front porch, and Billy told me I could start.

I wasn't exactly sure what details he'd heard, but it didn't matter. I knew he knew I'd kissed Matt. "Billy, I feel awful about what happened," I said. "I'm really sorry about what I did. I wish with all my heart that I could take it back and make it like it never happened."

Billy didn't say anything. He just sat there quietly and looked at me like he was taking in my side of things and trying to decide what he wanted to say.

I wanted him to say that he forgave me. "I'm so sorry," I said. Just knowing that I had a reason to be sorry made me upset. Tears were starting to form in the corners of my eyes. "Billy, I'm so, so sorry." I just looked at him. I didn't know how else to tell Billy I was sorry.

Billy was very matter-of-fact, like he'd

thought about and maybe rehearsed what he wanted to say. "April, I appreciate your apology, but we can't be us anymore. Not like we have been."

I wasn't sure what he was saying. "Are you breaking up with me?" I asked.

Billy nodded, and that's when I started crying. Tears were streaming down my face. I looked at Billy. I wanted him to do something sweet and Billy-like—bump my shoulder with his or wipe away my tears with a corner of his T-shirt or tell me not to worry and make a joke out of it.

But he didn't do any of those things. He just sat there while I cried, and when I was done, he stood up and handed me Gilligan's leash. He didn't say another word.

I took the leash and walked home. When I got to my room, I took off the bracelet Billy gave me and put it carefully in my jewelry box. I pulled my sleeve down to cover the tan line on my wrist where the bracelet had been.

I could hardly eat dinner. Everyone in my family could tell I was upset, but I couldn't bring myself to tell them why. How do you say you lost a best friend and a boyfriend?

After dinner, I went through the call log on my phone and added up the number of minutes Billy and I have talked this month: 532. All I could think about in the shower was how much I'm going to miss talking to Billy.

May and June came into my room before they went to sleep and got in bed with me. "Was someone mean to you?" asked May. "If they were, I'll beat them up."

June had her *Cinderella* book, which she loves. "Will you read to me?" she asked.

May and June curled up on either side of me. As I started to read the book, my tears fell on the pages. When I finished the story, May hugged me and June kissed me on the cheek. At least they still love me.

I'm not sure who else does.

11:42 P.M.

I must have fallen asleep with the light on, because Dad just came in and kissed me good night. He asked me if there's anything I'd like to talk about with him. I told him no. I can't talk to Dad about this. I can't tell my dad why Billy broke up with me or that Brynn isn't speaking to me and that no one on the dance team likes me anymore.

I hug Rat. My only friend is a bear who looks like a rat that was given to me by a boy who broke up with me.

Here's my heart and soul, please grind them into hamburger and enjoy.

—*Meredith Grey*

Halloween, 4:52 P.M.
In bed

I haven't written all week because I haven't had anything to write about. Nothing has changed since the last time I wrote.

Brynn isn't talking to me. Well, that's not entirely true. If she has to say something to me, like in school, she does. But she doesn't call or text or ask me if I want to hang out. And she hasn't said a word about her party tonight, which I know means I'm officially uninvited.

Things with Billy aren't any better. I've tried calling and texting a bunch of times, but he hasn't picked up any of my calls or responded to my texts.

They don't sit with me at lunch anymore. And to make matters worse, every time I see them at school, they're together. I don't even want to think about what they're talking about when I'm not with them. They're probably bonding over being mad at me. I'm sure Billy is upset (actually, I'm not so sure), and Brynn is there to comfort him. I can just hear what she's been saying to him.

"I know how hurtful this is. She was supposed to be my best friend, and she's been spilling her secrets to someone else." I'm sure she's also told Billy that she tried to warn me about Emily, but I wouldn't listen. Then she probably said something to Billy about how I don't always have the best judgment when it comes to people. There's no telling where the conversation went from there. It hurts my head just thinking about it.

Things in dance are bad too. I've tried to talk to Chloe and explain to her what really happened, but every time I try, she shakes her head or walks away like she doesn't want to hear what I have to say. I talked to my "big sister," Mady, about it, but all Mady said is that I should just focus on dancing. So that's what I've been doing, but I haven't enjoyed it.

I keep thinking about Gaga and her Happiness Movement. I wanted this year to be a good one, so I tried to be positive. But that didn't do much good. I guess you could argue that I did something that wasn't so positive when I kissed Matt. But does a person have to be positive all the time to stay happy? Can a girl make a mistake without her life falling apart?

Apparently not.

5:48 P.M.
Still in bed

May and June came into my room to show me their costumes. May is a pirate, and June is a goblin. Mom is taking them trick-or-treating.

"Do you want to come along?" asked May.

"Yeah," said June. "Come with us."

I told them I feel sick, which I do. I'm sick about what a mess my life is.

6:17 P.M.

I'm at home.

6:18 P.M.

Alone.

6:19 P.M.

On Halloween.

6:21 P.M.

In bed.

7:07 P.M.

My friends are at Brynn's party, which started at 7:00, and I'm home alone. In bed. Did I already say that? Sometimes when I'm upset, I get repetitive.

8:50 P.M.

May and June are back. May dumped her pumpkin full of candy on my bed and told me I could pick three pieces, just no Reese's, Snickers, Milky Ways, Nestlé Crunches, Hershey bars, M&Ms, Sweet Tarts, Smarties, or Three Musketeers, which basically only leaves Dum Dums, Jolly Ranchers, and weird no-name brands of candy.

Then June dumped her candy on my bed and literally repeated May's off-limits list of candy in perfect order. If I wasn't in such a horrific mood,

I'd actually be impressed.

I just picked a green Jolly Rancher.

Jolly fun night. Not really.

My one regret in life
is that I'm not someone else.

—*Woody Allen*

As far as my life goes, all the days are the same. Except today was different. It was worse. Everyone at school was talking about Brynn's party and how amazing it was. And to make things even worse, people were also talking about why I wasn't there.

During PE, I overheard Kelly Blake talking to Julia Lozano.

"I heard Brynn didn't invite her to the party because they're not friends anymore," Kelly said.

"They've been friends forever," Julia said.

"I know," said Kelly. "But you heard what happened, didn't you?" Then Kelly started whispering to Julia, so I couldn't hear what they were saying. But I didn't need to hear it. Before the party, some people at school knew what

124

happened, but by the end of the day, it was all over Faraway Middle School.

The only thing that could have been worse is if it had been in our school newspaper.

I don't even want to think about that possibility.

Monday, November 4, 6:04 P.M.

Today was the same as all my days have been lately.

BAD.

Tuesday, November 5, 8:17 P.M.

I thought I was depressed, so I read about it online.

Clinically, I don't seem to be exhibiting most of the symptoms. So I Googled semi-depressed, which is what I thought I might be, but I guess there's really no such thing. There's something like it called dysthymic, but the description was too long to read about, and it's probably not what I am anyway.

What I know I am is upset about my life. And no one seems to care.

Dad has tried to help. He really has. I know

he could tell something was wrong the night that Billy and I broke up. He's tried several times since then to get me to talk to him, but I haven't. Tonight, he brought home my favorite pie, key lime, from the diner.

It was sweet of him. But it didn't cheer me up.

Wednesday, November 6, 9:02 P.M.

Today at dance practice, Ms. Baumann went through the schedule of dances we're doing the night of the show. She talked for a long time about each jazz, ballet, hip-hop, and contemporary dance in our program. She went through the list of group dances, ensembles, and solos. "Girls, we have a lot of work to do. I don't think I need to remind you that the show is three weeks from today."

"You definitely don't need to remind us!" said Sarah Feinberg.

Everyone started laughing when she said it. Even Ms. Baumann smiled. She knows everyone is super excited about it.

Everyone but one person.

It's going to be a long three weeks.

Saturday, November 9, 2:45 P.M.
Just back from practice

Our costumes for the show came in, and this morning after practice, Ms. Baumann had everyone try them on. The other girls were laughing and joking around. It reminded me of the day the costumes came in before our first competition. For some reason, what Emily said when I'd asked Mady about wearing a padded bra came to mind. I'd been part of the joking around that day.

Sadly, a lot has changed since then.

Wednesday, November 13, 8:45 P.M.

Tonight when I got home from dance practice, I walked next door to Matt's house and rang his doorbell. I haven't spoken to him (aside from him checking out my boobs at the pep rally) since we kissed.

I wanted to know what he had to say about what happened. When I rang the bell, Matt opened the door. I just stood there for a minute because I hadn't planned what I was going to say if he answered.

He smiled at me. "What's up, California?" he asked.

It kind of pissed me off that he looked so happy when I felt so miserable. "Can we talk?"

Matt nodded, and I followed him into his backyard. We sat down under a tree. We both just sat there for a long time, and neither one of us said anything.

Finally, Matt looked at me. "California, you got something you want to say?"

I had no idea what was going to come out of my mouth until I opened it. "Did you know that Billy and I broke up?" I asked him.

Matt didn't really acknowledge if he knew that or not. "I'm sorry," he said.

Hearing him say he was sorry made me feel worse. It was like all the anger I'd felt since Emily told the world what I'd told her bubbled to the surface. It wasn't Matt's fault, but I needed somebody to be mad at. "We broke up because he found out what happened." I figured Matt was smart enough to know I meant what happened between us.

"How did he find out?" Matt asked.

I knew what was coming next. If I told Matt that I told Emily and she told the rest of the world, Matt was going to say he told me our kiss should be our secret. But I couldn't help myself. I'd been holding in so much for so long and I needed him to know what happened. I told him everything about Emily, Brynn, Billy, the girls on the dance team, and the kids at school.

I waited for Matt to do an I-told-you-so thing. But he didn't. He listened while I went on and on, and when I was done, he just looked at me with his big blue eyes. "That sucks," he said. Then he just sat there looking at me like it was an invitation to keep talking if I wanted to.

So I did. "When you kissed me, you said you liked me."

I regretted saying it the minute the words left my mouth. Especially the way I said it. It was more of a statement than a question, which made it hard for Matt to answer.

But his response surprised me. He reached over and squeezed my hand. "April, I'm sorry you're upset," he said, like he really meant it. Then he stood up and looked toward his house like the conversation was over and it was time for him to go back inside.

His apology didn't give me any of the answers I was looking for, but somehow it made me feel better.

When you're finished changing,
you're finished.

—*Ben Franklin*

Friday, November 22, 9:47 P.M.

Tonight we went to Gaga's house for dinner. Right when we got there, she made everyone sit down in the living room and said she had an announcement to make. All the grown-ups were looking at each other kind of nervously, like here we go again. Most grandmas announce they knitted a new sweater or they're taking the family on a cruise. But there was no telling what Gaga was going to say.

In her usual fashion, she didn't make us wait long.

"When I put my pants on, I have a muffin top," Gaga announced to her entire family as well as her lifelong best friend, Florence, and Mr. Sherman (her neighbor, who she claims is only a friend, but I think by the way he looks at her, he hopes it might be more).

I couldn't believe she even knew the word, but she did. And to make matters worse, she lifted up her blouse and showed everyone what she was talking about. I thought my Uncle Dusty was going to be sick. My Uncle Drew had to look away. To be honest, I didn't think it was possible to have a muffin top when you wear pants with an elastic waistband, but it is.

"I view this as a positive thing," Gaga said when she was done with her demonstration.

I wasn't sure how having a roll of fat hanging over the top of your pants was a positive thing, but Gaga said her muffin top is a call to action. "Ladies and Gentlemen," she said like she was talking to a studio audience. "Effective immediately, I am going on a health kick."

She motioned to the buffet in the dining room. "The chicken tonight will be lightly, not deep fried. And instead of mashed potatoes, we will be having broccoli and salad."

Then she picked up a Sports Authority bag and plunked it on the coffee table. "And I will be taking up jogging." She dug into the bag and pulled out a pair of running shoes, some shorts and shirts, and a pedometer.

Mr. Sherman put his fingers in his mouth and whistled. He might like the idea of Gaga cruising the streets of Faraway in a pair of Nike shorts, but it was more than I could bear. It was clear my cousin Amanda, who is in sixth grade but acts like she's in tenth, felt the same way, because she gave me the as-the-oldest-grand-daughter-it's-your-job-to-set-her-straight look.

So I said, "Gaga, aren't you kind of old to make such a radical change in your life?"

I probably should have taken a more scientific approach and said something like, "Have you checked with your doctors? Maybe you should just walk the mall with the other grandmas."

But I didn't do that, and when I said it, Gaga looked at me square on and said, "When you're finished changing, you're finished." Then, while everyone else was eating chicken and broccoli and salad, Gaga gave me a very long speech about how if you don't like the way things are, you should do something about them.

Gaga loves nothing more than an oppor-tunity to impart what she calls her "vast stores of wisdom based on years of experience," which just means that by the time she was done with me, my lightly fried chicken was freezing cold.

10:32 P.M.

I can't sleep. I keep thinking about what Gaga said to me.

Even though she's strange in lots of ways, I think she's right when she said someone should do something about things if they don't like the way they are. I felt better after I talked to Matt. I don't like the way things are with Billy or Brynn or the girls on the dance team. I know I need to do something to make things better.

I just don't know what that something is.

Saturday, November 23, 1:45 P.M.
Just home from the diner

This morning, I went to dance practice. It was our last Saturday practice before the fall show, which is on Wednesday. It should be such an exciting night, and I don't want the other girls on the team to still be ignoring me. I don't want Billy and Brynn to still be mad at me either.

We've hardly spoken for a month, and I miss my friends.

So when I finished dance practice, I went to the diner to talk to Dad. He's always been the person I talk to when I have a problem. Before he opened the diner last year, he wrote an advice column in the Faraway paper, so I have to believe he knows what he's doing when it comes to helping people with their problems.

When I got to the diner, Dad was busy with the lunch crowd, but when he saw me, I know he could tell it was important because he asked his assistant manager, Hal, to keep an eye on things. He took me back to his office and closed the door.

Dad sat down behind his desk. "What can I do for you, April?" he asked.

I looked around Dad's office. It's crammed with papers and boxes, which give it a very homey, lived-in feel that I like. There are quotes and recipes and pictures of pies taped to the walls. Dad keeps a bowl of Tootsie Rolls on his desk. I unwrapped one and started sucking on it. I wasn't sure what to say.

Sometimes Dad is like a mind reader. He

smiled at me in an understanding way. "Why don't you start at the beginning," he said softly.

So I did. I took a deep breath and told Dad everything that happened with Matt and Billy and Brynn and Emily and Chloe, and how everyone on the dance team is mad at me and that it feels like my whole life was going so well and then it fell apart and that even though I know it sounds dramatic, I don't feel like I'll ever be happy again, at least not in Faraway. Then I told Dad I don't want things to be the way they are. "I just don't know what to do to change them," I said.

Dad made a little tent with his fingers and put them over his lips like he was thinking. He was quiet for a long time. Even though he hadn't said anything yet, it felt good just getting everything off my chest.

Finally, he started talking. "April, you made a mistake. Your actions hurt other people."

I didn't need Dad to remind me of that. I could feel tears welling up in my eyes. But he kept talking. "Part of life is making mistakes. How you handle your mistakes makes the difference."

"I tried to apologize to Billy and to Brynn

and to Chloe, but no one wanted to accept my apology," I explained to Dad.

He nodded like he got what I was saying. "Sometimes people just need a little time before they're ready to hear what you have to say. It sounds like it has been a while now, and I think if you talk to your friends again, tell them how badly you feel, and sincerely apologize, they'll be open to listening."

I shook my head. "I don't see how time changes things," I said to Dad.

When I said that, Dad pointed to a piece of paper tacked up to the wall behind him. I read the piece of paper he was pointing to. *Let time be your best friend.*

It's one of Dad's favorite quotes. I'd read it dozens of times before, but it never meant anything to me. Hopefully, I can make time my best friend . . . or it will be the only friend I have.

4:48 P.M.
Just home from getting ice cream with Brynn

When I left the diner, I went to Brynn's

house. I could tell she was surprised to see me. "Do you want to go for ice cream?" I asked.

It's what we've always done when we need to talk, so I was happy Brynn agreed to go. On the way to the Cold Shack, neither one of us said much. When we got our hot fudge sundaes and sat down, I started talking first. "I've had a lot of time to think about what happened, and I know I really hurt you."

Brynn winced like she'd actually been in pain.

"Brynn, I'm really sorry," I said. "About everything."

"I just don't understand why you'd kiss Matt after everything that happened last summer. I don't see how you could have done that to Billy," she said. "And I really don't get why you would have talked to Emily about it and not me."

"I don't know why I kissed Matt," I told Brynn. "The truth is that it just happened." It was hard to find the words to explain. "I get confused whenever I'm around Matt," I told Brynn.

She looked at me in kind of a blank way when I said that, like she didn't really get my confusion. I wasn't sure I could say anything that would get Brynn to understand, but I tried. "The reason I didn't tell you is because I knew how you would react."

That definitely wasn't the right thing to say.

Brynn shook her head in a sad way. "April, you practically dumped me when you made the dance team. You hurt me, and you hurt Billy too."

I didn't see what Billy had to do with this. Just hearing her say his name made me mad. Even though I had gone to apologize to Brynn, right then I knew I had to say the things I'd kept in the last time we talked.

"Brynn, I was upset too. I was hurt that you didn't even congratulate me when I made the team. As my best friend, you could have at least been a little bit happy for me."

I hadn't planned to say what I did next, but it just came out. "I've also been upset because part of me feels like you have a thing for Billy. A more-than-a-friend thing."

Brynn's eyes looked like they were about to pop out of her head. She'd never admit it, but I knew she knew I'd nailed it. I kept going. "It bothered me when you called him to watch us dance, and then you went and talked to him about me behind my back. Do you know how I feel every time I see the two of you together in school, laughing and talking?"

I could tell Brynn didn't like hearing that. She sat in her chair, unmoving, quiet for a long time. She looked down at her melting ice cream. "April, I'm sorry I wasn't happier for you when you made the team, but it was hard for me." She paused and then she said, "Billy and I have been friends for a long time."

I waited for her to say she only likes Billy as a friend, but she didn't. She just looked at me like it was my turn. I knew that was as much as I would get from Brynn.

"You're my best friend," I said. "I'm so sorry about everything I did that hurt you. I just hope things can go back to how they were."

"It might take some time," said Brynn. But she didn't look as mad as she had before.

I told her I understood, and we promised to be straight with each other. Then we hugged and ate our ice cream.

It was a start.

After lunch, I went over to Billy's house to talk to him.

Billy answered the door, and we both just stood there looking at each other and not saying anything. It was totally awkward. He's always so straightforward and honest with people, so I knew that's what I needed to be with him. "Billy, I'm really sorry about everything that happened," I said. My heart still hurt when I talked to him. We sat down on his front porch. "Not a day goes by that I don't think about it," I said. "If I could go back in time and do things differently, I would."

It was the truth.

"I appreciate that," said Billy. He bumped my shoulder with his, which I knew meant he really did accept my apology.

"You're not mad anymore?" I asked softly.

He shook his head and smiled at me for the first time in a long time. It felt good.

I took a deep breath. "I want to go back to how we were. I want to be April and Billy again,"

I said. I'd been thinking it all morning, but I hadn't been sure if I should say it. The moment just seemed right, so I did.

Billy sat there for a minute. Then he looked at me in a sad kind of way and shook his head. "We can't go back to how things were," he said softly. I could tell that part of him wanted that too, but most of him didn't.

It might not have been what I hoped for, but I guess I wasn't surprised. It was what I expected. "Friends?" I asked.

Billy nodded like he could agree to that.

I always try to balance the light with the heavy—a few tears of human spirit in with the sequins and fringes.

—*Bette Midler*

Today was the dress rehearsal for the dance team fall show. I had to talk to Chloe and try to straighten things out. I was going to do it when I got to the high school auditorium, where we were rehearsing for the show, but the minute I showed up, Ms. Baumann sent me to the dressing room and told me to get in costume for my first dance.

Everyone on the team was getting ready. Chloe was there, but she was surrounded by a bunch of other ninth graders who were all in the same dance. It wasn't the right time to talk to her. She was with all her friends. Plus, Ms. Baumann came in while we were getting dressed and told us it was time to start.

We went through all the dances in the first

half of the show. There were twelve of them including solos, ensembles, and the group dances. Anyone who wasn't dancing was sitting in an area backstage, and Ms. Baumann said there was to be absolutely no talking backstage when other girls were performing, so I couldn't talk to Chloe then.

When we went back to the dressing room to get ready for our second round of dances, Ms. Baumann came back with us and said that on show night, we would have exactly ten minutes to change during intermission, which meant there would be no time for fooling around. She timed us while we changed, and no one said a word. There was no way I could have talked to Chloe.

Then we went back onstage and went through the second round of dances. No breaks. No talking. Still no chance to talk to Chloe. When we finished, Ms. Baumann brought everyone onstage for the finale.

When we had gone through the whole show to Ms. Baumann's satisfaction, she sent us all to get out of our costumes and put them in the labeled bags she had provided so nothing got lost. Then she gave us a final talk about Wednesday night and putting our hearts and souls into the show. Finally, she said we could go.

It was late, and everyone started leaving the auditorium. It was my only chance. Chloe was walking out of the auditorium with three of her friends. I would have preferred to talk to her alone, but there was no way that was happening. I ran up to the group. "Chloe, can I talk to you?" I asked.

The girls stopped and looked at me. My stomach was in knots. All I could do was sincerely apologize, like Dad said, and hope for the best. "Chloe, I'm really sorry about what happened." I looked down at my shoes. "I know I hurt you. You told me you liked Matt. But honestly, things really didn't happen the way you heard it."

My chest felt tight. It was scary explaining it in front of her friends. "I wasn't secretly going out with Matt. I kissed him once. I hadn't planned to kiss him at all, and right away, I wished it hadn't happened." I clasped my hands together in front of me. It kind of made me look like I was praying. I guess I kind of was. "I feel terrible about the whole thing. I'm really sorry. I just want to be friends with everyone on the team again."

When I finished talking, Chloe's friends looked at her like they were waiting to see what she would say. I waited too. Her response surprised me. "It's OK," she said. "I've gotten to know Matt better. I'm not really into him anymore anyway."

I don't know why, maybe it was not having talked to her for so long or just knowing she understood, but I could tell I was about to cry. I tried to blink back my tears.

Chloe was sweet. "I get it," she said. "Thanks for apologizing." Then she gave me a hug. It made me cry more. The other girls looked at each other like they weren't sure what to say.

Chloe's friend Samantha wrapped an arm around me. "It's OK," she said, but I couldn't stop crying. Tears were rolling down my cheeks.

Chloe's friend Alex shook her head. "You have to stop crying," she said. "The last thing you want on performance night is puffy eyes."

Mya, this other girl, was nodding like she had the same thought.

That made me laugh. I probably looked like a crazy person, crying one minute and laughing the next. But I didn't care. It was the first time I've laughed in a long time, and it felt good.

Tuesday, November 26, 1:44 P.M.
Study hall

Today during lunch, I went up to Emily and asked her if we could talk. There were some things I had to say to her. I told her that I didn't understand how she could tell everyone my secret and that I thought we were friends. Then I told her that I talked to Chloe yesterday and that she forgave me for what happened.

But Emily just shrugged her shoulders and said she really didn't know what I was talking about, that she never told anybody anything. Then she said she had to go.

It's fine. If she wants to pretend like it never happened, that's her business.

Brynn was definitely right on this one.

Wednesday, November 27, 4:40 P.M.
In my bathroom
About to leave for the dance show

My hair is in a bun. My makeup bag is packed. My fingers are crossed.

I hope tonight goes well.

11:45 P.M.
In bed
I should be tired
But I'm not

Tonight was amazing in so many ways. I'm not even sure where to start. When I arrived in the dressing room, everyone was excited. All the older girls were helping the younger girls put the finishing touches on their makeup. One of the straps on my costume was crooked, so Mady adjusted it and safety-pinned it to the inside of my costume to make sure it didn't move during the show. "You doing OK?" she asked. I nodded and she smiled in a big-sisterly way.

Chloe helped me finish my makeup. While she was putting on my lipstick, she told me she never even really liked Emily. "From day one," she said in a low voice, "she thought she was better than anyone on the team, and we've all been here a lot longer than she has." Surprisingly, I didn't care so much how Chloe felt about Emily, I was just happy to feel like part of the team again.

Once we were all dressed, Ms. Baumann gave us what she called our final dancing orders. She said they're like marching orders if you're in the army and that we should perform tonight as seriously as if we were but also have fun.

Then she sent us to the area on the side of the stage where we would be waiting before our opening number. I peeked through the curtains. The auditorium was packed. It was standing room only. Then I heard the music start and saw the stage lights go on. It was showtime.

The opening dance was the scariest. It was a group dance, and as everyone on the team crossed the stage and took our places, I was conscious of every part of my body. All of Ms. Baumann's orders played like a loop in my head. *Shoulders back. Toes pointed. Arms extended.* There was so much to remember, but once the music started, I relaxed into it.

At intermission, we changed costumes backstage. "No talking!" Ms. Baumann barked at us. "And hurry!" Even though Ms. Baumann had everything organized, the area backstage was tiny. There were costumes and dancers everywhere. I don't know how we all managed to find what we needed and get changed, but we did.

The second half of the show flew by. The second dance I was in included the leaps I worked so hard on. I don't know if it was the energy of performing onstage or the happiness I was feeling about being on good terms with the team again, but when I leapt, I felt like I was soaring.

Then, before I knew it, it was time for the finale.

When we finished our last dance, the auditorium was thundering with applause. The show was such a success! The audience cheered and clapped for a long time when we went back onstage for our final bows.

When the curtain finally closed, everyone on the team was hugging and high-fiving. Ms. Baumann told us what a great job we had done and how proud she was. The team captains gave her a huge bouquet of flowers. I've never seen her so happy or excited. Everyone was that excited. It felt great to be part of something so impressive, especially after putting in so much hard work.

Then, suddenly, the night was over. Sort of. One more thing happened that made my night. As I was packing up to go home, Billy and Brynn came backstage.

"Congratulations!" Brynn said. She hugged me. "You did an amazing job."

I hugged her back. I know it wasn't easy for her to say that. It was really sweet.

And Billy gave me flowers. Pink roses. "For you," he said as he handed them to me.

I must have looked a little too excited because he added, "They're friendship roses." I knew he didn't want me to misinterpret their meaning. I wanted to cry. Not because he gave me flowers or because they were pink, but because the two of them had both come to see me dance.

As great as everything that happened tonight felt—the show, the applause, the praise from Ms. Baumann, being a real part of the team—none of it could come close to the feeling of knowing that Billy and Brynn and I are all friends again.

If you want to be happy, be.

—*Leo Tolstoy*

Thanksgiving, 6:17 P.M.
In Dad's office at the Diner

We always have Thanksgiving at Gaga's house, but this year, Dad said he wanted to start a new tradition and have it at the diner. Gaga agreed, but only because Dad said he would use all of her favorite recipes. As it turned out, Gaga was waiting outside the diner early this morning when Dad, May, and I showed up to start cooking. She told Dad she wanted to be his "sous-chef," which I know meant she wanted to keep an eye on how he was doing things. But Dad was a good sport and said he was happy to have the extra help in the kitchen.

So today, my entire extended family, the ladies from Gaga's Happiness Movement, and Mr. Sherman all packed around a long table in the diner for Thanksgiving lunch. Dad cooked all of Gaga's traditional recipes, with her help, plus a few things he added to the menu, including crawfish beignets and lobster pie.

When I saw what he was cooking, I said, "Dad, those foods bring back some bad memories for me."

But Dad laughed and told me not to worry. "Today I'm the cooker, not the eater," he said. I felt kind of bad when he said that, and I told him he should eat too. Dad patted his belly (which has definitely gotten bigger since he opened a restaurant) and told me he doesn't have a problem in that department.

One of the things I always like best about Thanksgiving is that everyone is usually in a pretty good mood. But today, everyone was particularly happy.

The ladies from the Happiness Movement were happy, but I guess they always are.

Mr. Sherman, who seems happy whenever he's around Gaga, looked especially happy.

Even my uncles, Dusty and Drew, were happy. They said it was because we were all together as a family. Truthfully, I think they were just glad they were going home after lunch to watch football, which is something that never happened when lunch was at Gaga's house because she always made everyone stay for a family Scrabble tournament.

My cousins (with the exception of Harry) were happy because Dad said we could hang out in his office until lunch was ready. It's a cool place to hang out, so we sat in there for a long time, just eating Tootsie Rolls and talking.

My mom and her sisters were happy. They all had on matching turkey sweaters that Gaga had knitted for them. You wouldn't catch me dead in one of those sweaters, but they seemed to like them. They were smiling and taking group pictures with Gaga, who looked happier than anybody. Kind of strangely happy.

"Do you think she's been smoking something?" my cousin Harry asked me.

I'd kind of been wondering the same thing myself. She's a founding member of the Happiness Movement, so happy is to be expected, but she was way beyond happy. She was giddy, laughing and talking and taking pictures and hugging everyone. Something seemed different about Gaga. And after lunch, I found out what that something was.

When we were all done eating (what I'm sure was the largest and most delicious Thanksgiving lunch in the state of Alabama), Gaga tapped her spoon on her glass to get everyone's attention. "I'd like to make a toast," she said. Then she talked for a long time about the meaning of life and happiness.

It felt more like a speech than a toast, but then Gaga raised her glass and said, "Life is all in how you look at things. You can view your glass as half empty or half full or, better yet, all the way full."

Then she looked at Mr. Sherman, who was sitting next to her. "I have wonderful news. Willy has asked me to marry him, and I said yes!"

I thought my mom was going to pass out. Everyone looked shocked.

"That's disgusting," my cousin Amanda whispered to me.

But Gaga assured everyone that she was

exceedingly happy about this development, and Mr. Sherman, who said we should all call him Willy, said he was happy too.

So everyone got up and started hugging Gaga. We all gave Willy nice, firm handshakes, and my uncles patted him on the back and wished him well.

While everyone was crowded around Gaga looking at the ring on her finger, which she'd kept hidden in her pocket until she'd made her announcement, I saw my Uncle Dusty look at my Uncle Drew, roll his eyes, and make finger circles around the side of his head like Gaga was a crazy lady and he couldn't imagine what was next.

I couldn't either. I thought about how I felt when I started eighth grade. I was so convinced there was an old me and a new me. I wanted to believe that if I stayed positive everything would be great. I had so much to be happy about—an amazing boyfriend, a great best friend, making the dance team.

Things seemed almost too good to be true.

Then I kissed Matt, told Emily, she told

everyone else, and everything fell apart with Billy and Brynn and the girls on the team. One day my life seemed great, and the next day it was a disaster. I think part of the problem was that I got so wrapped up in how cool it was to be around the older girls on the team and Emily that I guess I kind of forgot how to be me.

Things are better now. They're not perfect. But they're mostly good. Brynn and I are friends again. Billy and I seem to be getting back to normal too. Part of me wishes he was still my boyfriend, but another part of me is just relieved we're friends. And I feel like part of the dance team again, and the show was amazing.

Being friends with Emily didn't turn out the way I thought it would, but at least now I know she's not someone I can trust.

And then there's Matt. I don't know if I should put him in the good or the bad category. I'm never sure about Matt. I guess he falls somewhere in between.

And maybe that's what life is like. There are times when life is good and times when it can be horrible. The good phase might last a day or a

week or a month or, if you're lucky, maybe longer. But at some point, there's going to be some
bad sprinkled in. And when there is, I think
Gaga actually had it right.

It's all in how you look at things.

About the Author

Laurie Friedman was on the gymnastics team in middle school and high school, but her real passion was and still is for dance. She identifies with April Sinclair not only in her love of dance but also in her small-town Southern roots, her questions about karma, and her adolescent confusion over two boys she liked for different reasons.

Laurie Friedman has written more than thirty books for young readers, including *Can You Say Catastrophe?*, the first book in The Mostly Miserable Life of April Sinclair series. She is also the author of the award-winning Mallory series as well as many picture books, including *I'm Not Afraid of this Haunted House*; *Love, Ruby Valentine*; *Thanksgiving Rules*; and *Back to School Rules*. She lives in Miami with her family. You can find Laurie B. Friedman on Facebook, Pinterest, and Twitter, or at www.lauriebfriedman.com.